Using Informational Text to Teach
The Great Gatsby

OTHER BOOKS BY THE AUTHORS

Connecting Across Disciplines: Collaborating with Informational Text

Using Informational Text to Teach A Raisin in the Sun

Using Informational Text to Teach To Kill a Mockingbird

Using Informational Text to Teach *The Great Gatsby*

AUDREY A. FISCH AND SUSAN R. CHENELLE

ROWMAN & LITTLEFIELD
Lanham • Boulder • New York • London

Published by Rowman & Littlefield
A wholly owned subsidiary of The Rowman & Littlefield Publishing Group, Inc.
4501 Forbes Boulevard, Suite 200, Lanham, Maryland 20706
www.rowman.com

Unit A, Whitacre Mews, 26-34 Stannary Street, London SE11 4AB

Copyright © 2018 by Audrey A. Fisch and Susan R. Chenelle

All rights reserved. No part of this book may be reproduced in any form or by any electronic or mechanical means, including information storage and retrieval systems, without written permission from the publisher, except by a reviewer who may quote passages in a review.

British Library Cataloguing in Publication Information Available

Library of Congress Cataloging-in-Publication Data Is Available

ISBN 978-1-4758-3101-6 (paperback : alk. paper)
ISBN 978-1-4758-3102-3 (electronic)

∞™ The paper used in this publication meets the minimum requirements of American National Standard for Information Sciences—Permanence of Paper for Printed Library Materials, ANSI/NISO Z39.48-1992.

Printed in the United States of America

The authors and publisher wish to thank those who have generously given permission to reprint material.

> Excerpts from "Exploding wealth inequality in the United States" by Emmanuel Saez and Gabriel Zucman. Equitable Growth. Reprinted by permission of the authors. All rights reserved.
>
> Excerpts from "Does money make you mean?" by Paul Piff. TEDxMarin. Reprinted with permission. All rights reserved.
>
> Excerpts from "Newspaper Coverage of the 1919 Black Sox Scandal" by Stuart Dezenhall. Reprinted by permission of the author. All rights reserved.

Contents

Preface ix
Acknowledgments xix
How to Use This Book xxi

Unit 1: Why Should We Care about Economic Inequality?   **1**

Emmanuel Saez and Gabriel Zucman: "Exploding wealth inequality in the United States"   15

David Vandivier: "What Is The Great Gatsby Curve?"   21

Chapters 1, 6, and 8

Unit 2: What Is Tom Buchanan Worried About—Is Civilization "Going to Pieces"?   **37**

Lothrop Stoddard: *The Rising Tide of Color Against White World-Supremacy*   50

Kenneth L. Roberts: *Why Europe Leaves Home*   55

Chapters 1, 2, 4, 7, and 9

Unit 3: Does Money Make People Such as Tom Mean?   **71**

Paul Piff: "Does money make you mean?"   84

Chapters 2, 6, and 8

Unit 4: Who Is to Blame in the Black Sox Scandal and in *Gatsby*? 101

"Eight White Sox Players Are Indicted on Charge of Fixing 1919 World Series; Cicotte Got $10,000 and Jackson $5,000" 115

Stuart Dezenhall: "Newspaper Coverage of the 1919 Black Sox Scandal" 120

Chapters 4 and 9

Unit 5: Everyone Is Drinking, So Why Does Prohibition Matter in *Gatsby*? 133

Eighteenth Amendment 144

The National Prohibition Act (The Volstead Act) 146

"Making a Joke of Prohibition in New York City" 149

Chapter 7 or any time

Writing and Discussion Rubrics 161

About the Authors 167

Tables and answers for all sections are available for download on the series website: www.usinginformationaltext.org.

Preface

USING INFORMATIONAL TEXT

As we complete work in 2017 on our fourth volume in the *Using Informational Text* series, the 2013 implementation of the Common Core seems a very long time ago. Will the Common Core endure, either in its own right or in the form of revised and renamed state standards? Will teachers continue to try to prepare students to read and grapple with a wide variety of texts and text types?

We hope so.

At the same time, bigger questions loom. How will our approach to the humanities, particularly to the teaching of literature, change in a world in which vocationally focused and STEM-centered education dominates? What effects will social media, the proliferation of unfiltered and fake news, disinformation, and distrust of traditional media have on the next generation of young learners? And what, more broadly, is the future of public education in the United States?

For us, these questions drive even deeper our conviction that our foremost task is to develop our students to be skilled, empathetic, critical readers of literature and of a variety of texts. We need our young people to be able to read discerningly as they grapple with both standardized tests and political doublespeak. We need them to make connections with history, to grasp the social and political complexity of stories and language, and to think about the relationship between texts and contexts.

THE GREAT GATSBY

Our series began with *Using Informational Text to Teach* To Kill a Mockingbird (2014). We moved from there to *Using Informational Text to Teach* A Raisin in the

Sun (2016), with a side journey through a discussion of fruit fly experiments, male aggression, and *Lord of the Flies*, in *Connecting Across Disciplines: Collaborating with Informational Text* (2016), our guide to cross-disciplinary collaboration.

When we turned to the question of what literary text to take on next, F. Scott Fitzgerald's *The Great Gatsby* was an obvious choice. The novel is at or near the top of various lists of the texts most commonly taught in high school in the United States. It is appealing to language arts teachers for many reasons: it's relatively short; it's chock-full of the kind of literary symbols and literary language that so many English teachers find compelling; and it engages that most basic American theme, the American Dream.

But for young students today, what does *Gatsby* signify?

Audrey surveyed some of her students, college students embarking on an English major, about their experience with *Gatsby* in high school. Some of their answers are worth quoting at length:

> *Student one*: Honestly, I never finished Gatsby. I read half of it and then gave up because I just did not enjoy it. I sparknoted the rest of the novel to get by in class. I did not like the hype surrounding it at the time either, because the movie with Leonardo DiCaprio had just come out and everyone was making it out to be something amazing and it just fell short for me. The only theme that I can vaguely remember about Gatsby was the green light across the water holding a meaning deeper than it just being a green light. But, I do not remember what the deeper meaning was.

> *Student two*: I did study Gatsby in high school and though I vaguely remember what was discussed, what I do remember is what motivated Gatsby, the "bootlegger," to deceive everyone, including himself—Daisy (the love of his life)—and his friends in order to live up to societ[y's] expectations. In the end, those lies lead up to his fatality.

> *Student three*: Yes, we studied it my junior year of high school. Yes, I read the novel, but I do not remember much of it. It was pleasurable in some areas, but difficult to read alone at first. I enjoyed discussing it in class. There was the American dream theme, chasing lost dreams, and the wealthy upper class society. We also talked about there being a lot of symbolism. Other than that, I don't recall much.

The green light, the love story, the lies, and the American Dream—these are some of the ways Fitzgerald's novel stands out in the minds of three students who read some, if not all, of the assigned text. Keep in mind that these responses are among the strongest, culled from students who selected a major in English in college. Clearly, for many others, *Gatsby* represents an even more vague memory of a half-read text about ultra-rich people and their loves and lies, along with some symbols such as the green light.

It might be worth noting that our critical emphasis as English teachers on the green light and symbolism in *Gatsby* is no accident. As Richard Anderson writes in "Gatsby's Long Shadow: Influence and Endurance," "*The Great Gatsby* came into critical favor at the height of the practice of the New Criticism, one emphasis of which was close reading of symbols and theme" (Anderson 1985, 28). New Criticism, however, is only one mode of literary criticism and one way to respond to Fitzgerald's novel. Moreover, as the comments indicate, it doesn't suffice either to plumb the depths of Fitzgerald's novel or to capture the interest of students today.

Our emphasis on the green light, however, cannot be blamed for the unremarkable reaction to *Gatsby* on the part of our students. These student responses about high school experiences with *Gatsby* are hardly exceptional. We know that students today are more and more likely to be consulting *Spark Notes* or other online guides rather than reading the assigned literary texts. If you haven't already done so, watch Penny Kittle's "Why Students Don't Read What's Assigned in Class" video (2010). Audrey's formerly nonreading students are no exception.

And just as disturbing as the fact that students who self-select as English majors have eschewed the assigned literary reading in high school is the vague and foggy way in which students articulate their takeaways from reading *Gatsby*. Clearly, our purpose in reading this, like other literary texts, is obscure or dimly perceived by students. As Cris Tovani (2000) notes, it is all too common that without a clear purpose for reading, even relatively diligent and well-intentioned students learn to "fake-read" early on, as she did, and are able to get by doing so all the way through high school (4–5).

We may think our purpose as teachers in the classroom is clear; we may think it's obvious to students what we hope they will take away from *Gatsby*, but typically this is not the case. Unless we foreground the big ideas and essential questions we hope to address in relation to the text (Wiggins and McTighe 2005; Burke 2010), students are likely to have little sense of the purpose of their reading.

Another point is worth considering about *Gatsby*: the disconnect between Gatsby's "wealthy upper-class society," as one of Audrey's students described it, and our increasingly diverse student populations. Stephanie Powell Watts (2017) describes the tension of being a "poor, small town, black girl" reader glimpsing the "rich, romantic, sophisticated, adult world" of *Gatsby* but also feeling repulsed by how this novel functions by "excluding and demeaning people of color, women, [and] the poor." This is a novel in which two African American men are dehumanized by their description as "two bucks" and then characterized as an animalistic threat, "the yolks of their eyeballs rolled toward us in haughty rivalry" (69).

Other characters employ the slur "kike" (34) to describe Jews; and Wolfsheim, the Jewish gangster, is described primarily in relation to his stereotypical Jewish nose.

A presumably poor child playing by the side of the road is described only as "a grey, scrawny Italian child" (26); no gender identification is necessary for this minor character who inhabits a world miles from Daisy's "beautiful . . . white girlhood" (19).

The language of class prejudice, racialism, and racial disruption is not found in isolated moments within *Gatsby*. The novel as a whole worries about what is happening in the new world of the twenties in which African American men can be driven by a white servant, Jews can tamper with baseball and the American economy, and vaguely nonwhite upstarts intrude more and more on the beautiful white world of the wealthy. Tom Buchanan articulates this view baldly: "if we don't look out the white race will be—will be utterly submerged" (13).

Little wonder, then, that some students who wade into the text may be repulsed, as was Stephanie Powell Watts, author of *No One Is Coming to Save Us*, a reimagining of *Gatsby*, by the sense that they are "not a member of the desired audience, that the story was not written for" them.

The irony, however, is that *Gatsby* is so very much, as Watts writes, a "book for our own time too, a time that is characterized by economic and racial fear, a time of great wealth for a few and great uncertainty for many." This 1925 novel may often be read as a historical glimpse at the gilded Jazz Age, but it even more brilliantly articulates the themes of our exact historical moment: hysteria about immigration and the decline of white America; income inequality at levels unseen since the twenties and a lack of opportunity for social mobility; anti-Semitism and concerns about the ways in which racial mixing has damaged the United States; bullying, incivility, entitlement, and lawlessness by those who hold power in society; and a broader culture of scapegoating, in which blame for society's ills is laid at the feet of the immigrant, the poor, or the Other.

Our research about and reading of *Gatsby* suggest that Fitzgerald's 1925 novel is the perfect text for this cultural moment, as it is a novel that explores the very issues of power and inequality that dominate the American landscape.

We hope that in pairing these informational texts with *Gatsby*, you will come to share our vision, and your students will find their way into memorable high school classroom experiences that move beyond explorations of potent symbols (that green light and those Eckleburg eyes) and into deep and critical examination of questions of power and social mobility in a vastly unequal world, questions that resonate strongly with the world and daily lives of our students today.

OUR UNITS

We begin with this question: Why Should We Care about Economic Inequality? *Gatsby*, after all, is a world utterly alien to our students. The characters are ultra-wealthy.

Their lives, full of fancy cars, polo ponies, and parties, bear little resemblance to most people's reality.

Our first unit begins with research by two Berkeley economics professors, Emmanuel Saez and Gabriel Zucman, who explore the wealth gap in the United States. They explore our economic climate in relation to history and make clear that the world of Gatsby and Tom Buchanan still closely mirrors the economic reality of some in the United States. In fact, as we write this in 2017, wealth inequality, in decline from the 1930s until the 1970s, most closely resembles conditions in the Roaring Twenties, with alarming consequences for American ideals of opportunity.

In fact, our second reading in this unit, by Obama White House Chief of Staff David Vandivier, explores economist Alan Krueger's idea of The Great Gatsby Curve, an illustration of the association between family wealth and economic mobility. Vandivier moves these ideas of inequality and mobility into a global comparison and discusses evidence that, in areas of the world where income inequality is higher, children from poor families are less likely to be able to move out of poverty.

Together, these two readings suggest that Gatsby's experience may be a dystopian parable. For a child born into poverty or modest means, such as James Gatz, the only way to wealth may be through crime.

Our second unit moves from issues of social mobility and economic inequality to another central feature of political discussion: immigration and nativism. For this unit, our essential question is: What Is Tom Buchanan Worried About—Is Civilization "Going to Pieces"?

Like many people in the United States today, Tom is worried about the diminution of American exceptionalism; and his language, and much of the language of the novel, is racially coded in ways that students may not immediately be able to decipher.

Fitzgerald is relatively explicit, however, in footnoting the cultural sources of Tom's ideology. Our two readings for this unit are drawn from two white nationalist texts Fitzgerald alludes to in *Gatsby*. The first comes from Lothrop Stoddard, whom Tom calls Goddard. Tom exclaims that "[c]ivilization's going to pieces" and asks Nick if he has "read 'The Rise of the Coloured Empires' by this man Goddard?" (12). The real title of the text by Stoddard is *The Rising Tide of Color Against White World-Supremacy*; and not only does Tom reference the text, but Fitzgerald also goes out of his way to drop Stoddard's name a second time in the course of the novel. Gatsby, as Fitzgerald gratuitously informs us, also owns "Volume One of the 'Stoddard Lectures'" (45), although the pages of Stoddard, like all of the books in Gatsby's library, remain uncut, to the amazement of the "middle-aged man, with enormous owl-eyed spectacles" (45) at Gatsby's party.

The insertion of Stoddard by name into *Gatsby* likely reflects Fitzgerald's recognition that Stoddard's ideas about the danger facing white civilization, both in Europe and the United States, were so mainstream. According to scholar Ronald Berman, Stoddard was a "household name" (1994, 25). His ideas about the threat of the "colored world" were even cited by President Harding in a speech in Birmingham, Alabama, on October 26, 1921. Harding said, "Whoever will take the time to read and ponder Mr. Lothrop Stoddard's book on *The Rising Tide of Colour* . . . must realise that our race problem here in the United States is only a phase of a race issue that the whole world confronts" (Berman 1994, 380–81).

We also include a piece from Kenneth L. Roberts, who wrote regularly for the well-known *Saturday Evening Post*, which Tom and Jordan read in chapter 2 of *Gatsby*. This second reading echoes Stoddard in worrying about the danger to white society posed by immigration and assimilation. Roberts, however, focuses specifically on Jewish immigrants as criminals, and this reading is particularly helpful in thinking about the stereotypical and anti-Semitic representation of Meyer Wolfsheim.

Together, the two readings in this section begin to unearth the racist and anti-Semitic underside of the glamorous world of *Gatsby*. The texts in this section give students specific language and historical context with which to discuss the cultural nativism and white supremacy featured in the novel. We hope students will begin to ask big questions about whether Fitzgerald is reflecting, endorsing, or critiquing these repugnant ideas with his text. Most of all, we hope this unit serves as a vehicle for critically informed conversations about immigration and nativism in contemporary political discourse.

Our third unit, Does Money Make People Such as Tom Mean?, turns to social psychology and some, at least superficially, amusing experiments involving Monopoly, popcorn and candy eating, and breaking the speed limit. Psychology and social behavior researcher Paul Piff, in excerpts from his TED Talk, has some darker concerns, however, about how wealth breeds greed, entitlement, and meanness. His talk and the interesting experiments he discusses provide a very different kind of context for some of the less-than-nice behaviors we see in *Gatsby*.

Piff's findings that money makes people mean resonate powerfully with the work of Emmanuel Saez and Gabriel Zucman discussed in unit 1, as the United States features such extraordinary levels of inequality. Given that *Gatsby* is such a bleak text, and one in which heroism, role models, and morality are in short supply, Piff's discussion about how researchers, wealthy individuals, and activists are working to combat the meanness augmented by economic and social inequality is a heartening coda to his research.

In our fourth unit, Who Is to Blame in the Black Sox Scandal and in *Gatsby*?, and our fifth unit, Everyone Is Drinking, So Why Does Prohibition Matter in *Gatsby*?, we turn to two now-distant historical events that are likely quite alien to our students. Our goal in these two units is to give students enough background so they can understand and think critically about how Fitzgerald is working off of and commenting on the historical realities of his day.

In the fourth unit, we unpack the 1919 Black Sox scandal with two very different accounts of the event. The first is an excerpt of a 1920 *New York Times* article on the indictment of the eight players for the White Sox who conspired with gamblers to fix the series, which includes testimony from one of the primary players involved. This piece ostensibly represents the facts of the case, but a second piece, from a 2012 sports journalism blog, casts some doubt on the overall accuracy of newspaper reports on the scandal at the time. Stuart Dezenhall focuses, in particular, on how the combination of anti-Semitism and the myth of the American baseball player shaped media coverage of the scandal, including which parties in the conspiracy were blamed and which were not.

Given that Fitzgerald assigns blame for the Black Sox scandal to his fictional Jewish gangster, Meyer Wolfsheim, the unit allows students to ponder again the ways in which *Gatsby* centers on a messy world full of conflict between whites and nonwhites (Jews and others, including the "gray, scrawny Italian child" [26], certainly were not considered white at the time of the novel).

Finally, with our fifth unit on Prohibition, we explore the historically specific ways in which the rich could, in the twenties, flout the rules and cheat, as they do in Paul Piff's experiments. Prohibition operates within *Gatsby* as one more arena of inequality, in which the rules of the ordinary world don't apply to those with power and money. Indeed, in *The War on Alcohol: Prohibition and the Rise of the American State*, Lisa McGirr (2016) offers a fascinating broader context for the ugly inequality of Prohibition enforcement that goes beyond the scope of our unit but is worth noting:

> [M]any Americans, and especially poor men and women, found themselves ensnared in one or more of Prohibition's webs, arrested, charged, fined, or incarcerated.... Prohibition policing differed by region, by rural or urban setting, and more especially by race, ethnicity, and class. An unprecedented glamor of the roaring twenties left the urbane elite sipping cocktails in swank, protected nightclubs from New York's Cotton Club to Chicago's Plantation Club, while [other] men ... died over a jug of whiskey. Uneven enforcement was the hidden reason the white, urbane upper-middle class could laugh ... while poor European immigrants, African-Americans, poor whites in the South, and the unlucky experienced the full brunt of Prohibition enforcement's deadly reality. (71)

The readings in this section allow students to understand some of the basic legal elements of Prohibition—including the ways in which the Eighteenth Amendment was distinctly vague on what exactly was prohibited and the National Prohibition Act (also known as the Volstead Act) created a complicated set of exemptions from Prohibition and a blueprint for corruption. We also include a newspaper piece from the *New York Times* that, in a jaunty and ironic tone, illustrates the specific climate of noncompliance with Prohibition in New York City and documents the well-known association of drugstores with bootlegging.

With this unit, students can begin to think through how and why the alcohol consumption at Gatsby's parties is fashionable and exciting, while Gatsby's drugstore ownership and bootlegging define him as disreputable and the appropriate object for Tom's disdain.

To be clear, our units are constructed to support your students' critical thinking about the issues that appear in *Gatsby*, not to tell them what to think about them. We hope that the readings and writing and discussion prompts we offer here will help them develop a richer context to draw from when considering how these issues play out not only in *Gatsby*, but in their own lives as well.

THE NECESSITY OF DIVERSE, CHALLENGING INFORMATIONAL TEXT

Novels have been deservedly praised as vehicles for developing empathy, the acute importance of which President Obama reminded us in his Farewell Address (2017). President Obama said, "if our democracy is to work in this increasingly diverse nation, then each one of us need[s] to try to heed the advice of a great character in American fiction—Atticus Finch—who said, 'You never really understand a person until you consider things from his point of view . . . until you climb into his skin and walk around in it.'"

This passage, a favorite for many teachers, comes at the beginning of chapter 4 in *To Kill a Mockingbird* (Lee 1982), when Atticus describes to Scout the practice of climbing into another's skin, or what we might today call radical empathy, as a "simple trick" (39). The political climate in 2017 suggests that nothing about this trick is simple.

Recent scholarship, including a 2013 study from The New School for Social Research, indicates that literary fiction helps our students build empathy, particularly the ability to understand "others' subjective states . . . [and] allows successful navigation of complex social relationships and helps to support the emphatic responses that maintain them" (Comer Kidd and Castano 2013, 377). And although so much of the focus is on cultivating so-called twenty-first-century skills such as communication and collaboration, critical thinking, and media literacy, our students need empathy, not just literacy skills and knowledge, to succeed.

At the same time, we argue for the role nonfiction can play in helping students cultivate critical thinking and empathy beyond the fictional worlds they encounter in literary fiction. We believe that our classrooms can be places where we help our students thoughtfully confront the sometimes ugly, contentious realities of their lives and the world around them as well. With Jocelyn A. Chadwick (2016), we think teachers must not turn away from difficult conversations about race, class, inequality, and social injustice.

We hope *Using Informational Text to Teach* The Great Gatsby will help you in that endeavor. Great texts, such as *Gatsby*, and the never-ending supply of interesting companion texts we can use to draw out the issues in *Gatsby*, give us a common language with which to have these classroom conversations. We can talk, via Fitzgerald and Emmanuel Saez and Gabriel Zucman, about the inequity of Jay Gatsby's limited opportunities for economic mobility. We can use Paul Piff to think about bullying and entitlement in *Gatsby*. And in so doing, we can use the power of literature and nonfiction to guide our students in important, difficult conversations.

Chadwick asks us to be led in these difficult conversations by the "curiosity and risk and daring and inquiry" (89) of today's students, who can and should be asking important new questions of the literary texts they read and the world around them. She articulates our views eloquently: our task is to make our classrooms "safe and trusted spaces for . . . difficult conversations" (91). We hope this volume will help you do so.

REFERENCES

Anderson, Richard. 1985. "Gatsby's Long Shadow: Influence and Endurance." In *New Essays on the Great Gatsby*, edited by Matthew J. Bruccoli, 15–40. New York: Cambridge University Press.

Berman, Ronald. 1994. *The Great Gatsby and Modern Times*. Urbana: University of Illinois Press.

Burke, Jim. 2010. *What's the Big Idea: Question-Driven Units to Motivate Reading, Writing, and Thinking*. Portsmouth, NJ: Heinemann.

Chadwick, Jocelyn A. 2016. "We Dare Not Teach What We Know We Must: The Importance of Difficult Conversations." *English Journal* 106(2): 88–91.

Comer Kidd, David, and Emanuele Castano. 2013. "Reading Literary Fiction Improves Theory of Mind." *Science* 342(6156): 377–80.

Common Core State Standards Initiative. 2010. *Common Core State Standards for English Language Arts and Literacy in History/Social Studies, Science, and Technical Subjects*. Washington, DC.

Fitzgerald, F. Scott. 2004. *The Great Gatsby*. New York: Charles Scribner's Sons, 1925. Reprint, New York: Scribner.

Kittle, Penny. 2010. "Why Students Don't Read What's Assigned in Class." *YouTube* video, 5:28, March 15. https://www.youtube.com/watch?v=gokm9RUr4ME.

Lee, Harper. 1982. *To Kill a Mockingbird*. New York: Harper & Row, 1961. Reprint, New York: Hachette Book Group.

McGirr, Lisa. 2016. *The War on Alcohol: Prohibition and the Rise of the American State*. New York: Norton.

Moffett, James, and Betty J. Wagner. 1991. *Student-Centered Language Arts, K–12*. New York: Heinemann.

Obama, Barack. 2017. "Farewell Address." Speech. Chicago, January 10.

Tovani, Chris. 2000. *I Read It, But I Don't Get It*. Portland, ME: Stenhouse.

Watts, Stephanie Powell. 2017. "I Love *The Great Gatsby*, Even If It Doesn't Love Me Back." *Lithub*, April 3. http://lithub.com/i-love-the-great-gatsby-even-if-it-doesnt-love-me-back/.

Wiggins, Grant, and Jay McTighe. 2005. *Understanding by Design*. Upper Saddle River, NJ: Pearson.

Acknowledgments

This series came about and has continued through conversations between the two authors about the exciting possibilities of the Common Core State Standards and our longstanding belief in the opportunities for informational text to help students think critically and deeply about both commonly taught canonical texts and the world in which we live.

We are immensely grateful to Tom Koerner, Carlie Wall, and the entire team at Rowman & Littlefield for being so supportive of our vision; we are especially thankful to Karen Ackermann for navigating the specific challenges of this volume.

We also are grateful for the institutional support we have had for this project. This includes the invaluable support of Frederick Smith, Laura Kortz, and James Brown at the Guarini Library at New Jersey City University.

Susan wishes to acknowledge valuable institutional support from Dean Erie Lugo and the Board of Trustees of University Academy Charter High School.

Audrey would like to acknowledge institutional support from New Jersey City University and her wonderful community there, including Debbie Bennett, Erik Morales, Winifred McNeill, Lourdes Sutton, Irma Maini, Allan De Fina, Alina Gharabegian, and Hilary Englert for many conversations about teaching and education. The outstanding students in Audrey's methods classes and alumni of the secondary English education program at NJCU have helped to shape this project in more ways than can be acknowledged here. Thanks, finally, to Max Flysch for sharing his many experiences in the language arts classroom and to Mark Flynn for his never-ending support.

Susan would like to acknowledge her generous and insightful colleagues and her students at University Academy Charter High School, from whom she learns every day. She also wishes to thank Sarah Tantillo for her feedback and conversations about the important role informational text plays in student literacy. Finally, she would like to thank her parents, Justin and Nancy Chenelle; and her partner, Ian Cook, for their unwavering, essential support.

Finally, we acknowledge the language arts teachers across the United States who work hard every day to make their classrooms places of substantive inquiry and lively engagement where students develop a love of literature and of learning.

How to Use This Book

This book is designed to make it easy for you to include informational text in your teaching of *The Great Gatsby*.

We have included a wide range of materials in terms of reading level, subject matter, length, and style of writing. Some materials are historical in orientation and offer background information and context to help your students make sense of Fitzgerald's historically specific and now quite historically distant text; others are more polemical and offer students a different kind of window into the text.

Read through the texts. Which will best fit your existing emphasis with *Gatsby*? Which will enable you to fill gaps in your students' knowledge or understanding? Which will help your students be excited about and connect with Fitzgerald's novel? Which will allow you to collaborate with a content area teacher in your school in order to make connections across the disciplines?

The answers to these questions will and should change year after year. Each year, balance your personal taste with the needs of your students and select different informational texts to incorporate into your teaching.

DIFFERENTIATION AND SUPPORTING ALL LEARNERS

In terms of accommodating the variety of students in our learning communities, think about how the variety of texts, topics, and types of traditional and nontraditional writing assignments and projects—many of which can be worked on in groups of students practicing their collaborative skills—can help you differentiate your classroom. You may want certain students to concentrate on prompts that focus solely on the informational text before tackling the challenge of connecting the informational reading(s) to *Gatsby*. You may decide, based on available time and your essential instructional goals, to modify what students produce in response to the writing prompts. Some students, for example, may produce only an outline of their arguments with the textual evidence they would use to support them.

You may allow your students the opportunity to choose from among the various units or the different texts within each unit as part of your differentiation. Some selections are longer and more challenging than others; certain students will find some selections more interesting. You may use a variety of selections to jigsaw your teaching to allow individual students and/or groups of students to take responsibility to "teach" the pieces to the class.

Perhaps you are concerned about how your struggling readers or English-language learners will do with these texts. We have witnessed firsthand how the supports in these units can help all students have successful and meaningful reading experiences. The pre-reading vocabulary exercises and the sidebar reading prompts support active reading and critical thinking and will build your students' confidence as they tackle these readings.

Indeed, higher-level texts and questions, which promote deeper engagement with big issues and a sense of purpose, can be easier, even when a student has some basic reading comprehension problems. A student might struggle with reading words on the page, but reading supports can remove barriers that might impede that critical thinking. In this way, we can engage all students, even those who have difficulty with reading and writing.

TEACHER'S GUIDE
Each section begins with a brief teacher's guide, in which we address the challenges and possibilities the featured informational text offers. The teacher's guide indicates which Common Core anchor standards are met by each discussion and writing activity.

The guide also includes suggested timing for integrating the informational text and discussion and writing activities into your teaching. All of the informational texts can be read without any knowledge of the novel, so you can begin your unit on *Gatsby* with an informational text as your hook, in this way provoking student interest and framing some of the issues you will focus on within the novel. Other activities in each unit, however, are better timed at particular moments in your students' reading of the text: to give students' context, to elicit discussion and reactions, and to enliven your students' responses.

ESSENTIAL QUESTIONS

Each article and writing activity begins with an essential question to guide study of the featured informational text. Following Grant Wiggins's backward-design model (2005, 110), we have designed the questions to enable teachers to

- *create* authentic inquiry into big ideas;
- *provoke* sustained thought and investigation;
- *require* the use of evidence and the consideration of alternate viewpoints;
- *promote* rethinking of assumptions;
- *produce* connections with personal experience and prior learning; and
- *allow* for the meaningful transfer of reading, thinking, speaking, listening, and writing skills.[1]

Our essential questions are designed, in other words, to create pathways into the informational texts and suggest connections between each informational text and *Gatsby*.

MEDIA LINKS

Within the teacher's guide, we have included a list of media links that connect with the topics and issues raised in these informational texts. These resources include online video and audio clips, full-length documentaries, and multimedia slideshows. We have provided descriptive detail about each resource (rather than listing specific URLs, as Web page addresses change so frequently), so you should be able to find it through any Internet search engine.

We encourage you to use these resources not just to build background knowledge for the informational texts and *Gatsby*, but in dialogue with the novel and the informational texts, so that students can "Integrate and evaluate content presented in diverse media and formats, including visually and quantitatively, as well as in words," as called for by the Common Core State Standards (CCSS) Reading Anchor Standard 7.

Certainly, some of us teach in technology-poor classrooms that make using multimedia texts challenging. But let's be clear how important this work is: the standards and many of our standardized assessments ask students to engage with audio and/or visual texts in relation to written texts. Reading text no longer refers only to reading words on paper.

Moreover, we see multimedia texts as important in two different ways.

First, these clips can produce high levels of engagement and painlessly prime students with background information, often in a matter of minutes. The wealth of material on YouTube includes many high-quality videos on any number of topics. A well-produced media clip, complete with catchy music or visual effects, has high appeal for this media-immersed generation. We should take the opportunities that multimedia texts offer to hook our students.

Second, although these multimedia texts are engaging, they are not simple. We need to teach our students to be active consumers of media. Too often, students assume a passive attitude toward media. Or we, as teachers, assume that they have a greater critical fluency with multimedia texts than with traditional texts. This is not necessarily the case. We need to teach our students to read these multimedia texts actively, asking questions about purpose and audience, about organization and evidence, and about textual features (which may mean camera angles, editing, lighting, music, special effects). They need to learn how and when to reread multimedia texts: a sixty-second video clip should be watched and rewatched, just like a poem or a piece of prose.

Our media suggestions, then, work to engage student interest and develop media literacy. Each of our units includes several suggestions for short audiovisual clips and/or photos that are well worth your effort in securing media access. If your school or district blocks YouTube, investigate the browser plugins that allow you to download videos.

Note: we haven't designed any of our discussion and writing questions around any of the multimedia texts because we were concerned about their long-term availability. But given the general nature of the current standardized assessment prompts, it's easy to design your own. Consider these stems when asking your students to compare and contrast one or two of our informational texts with a multimedia text.

- Write an essay analyzing the arguments about X. Base the analysis on the specifics, arguments, and principles put forth in the three sources you have studied.
- You have studied three sources on X. Write an essay in which you have explored X. Consider how the different authors present/represent X.
- Write an essay that contrasts the primary arguments in each text about X. Think about how each author supported his or her claim with reasoning and/or evidence.
- Write an essay comparing the information presented in each text. Use evidence from each text in your response.

VOCABULARY

Reading informational text poses challenges for our students in terms of both academic and domain-specific vocabulary, and the Common Core Language Standard places an increased emphasis on addressing these challenges. We have designed activities to help you meet your students' needs, to make the informational texts accessible, and to take advantage of the opportunities these texts provide for enhanced vocabulary acquisition and use.

Each section begins with a vocabulary warm-up that will facilitate understanding of challenging vocabulary prior to reading the text. We have crafted these activities not only to front-load challenging vocabulary, but to introduce concepts in the article. Discussion of these words in conjunction with the section's essential question can help promote students' interest, encourage them to ask their own pre-reading questions, and support their confidence.

The vocabulary questions are constructed to meet the needs of the Language Standard. Sections A and B address Anchor Standard 4 for Language, asking students to develop their ability to use context clues to determine the meaning of words in both multiple-choice and open-ended questions.

Section C asks students to deepen their knowledge and critical approach to language by learning to practice their dictionary skills (Anchor Standard 4 for Language) in relation to words that appear to be common but are used in uncommon, unfamiliar ways.

Section D asks students to use dictionaries to determine the meaning of a word and promotes authentic and engaging use of the word.

Section E involves using the words in different forms or with different endings, again to promote useful practice.

Section F gives students the opportunity to solidify their ownership of the vocabulary in original skits. The vocabulary skits are intended to create "massive practice" (Moffett and Wagner 1991, 10) so that your students work extensively with the new words in ways that are fun and meaningful.

This combination of exercises is intended to offer multiple opportunities to practice the vocabulary acquisition skills listed in the CCSS, based on the model for "rich" vocabulary instruction that moves "beyond definitional information" and works "to get students actively involved in using and thinking about word meanings and creating lots of associations among words" outlined by Beck, McKeown, and Kucan (2002, 73).

The vocabulary questions can be used in any number of ways. Students can complete all of the questions individually as homework; however, this is our least favorite approach to this material. We prefer to use these activities in class and in groups, so that students work together on the assigned sets of questions, answer them, and then share their thinking with their peers.

In addition, vocabulary-related questions recur in the sidebars alongside the articles as readers are asked to use their vocabulary knowledge to translate the informational text into their own words. Follow-up vocabulary questions are included in the "Check for Understanding" section after each article to assess students' comprehension of key vocabulary words as well as their ability to apply the vocabulary acquisition skills.

THE INFORMATIONAL READINGS
Each informational text or set of texts is presented to your students with a number of features.

First, we created a brief introduction to the unit as well as to each reading in the unit, so students can learn a bit about the texts they are going to read. When a unit contains more than one text, you may choose to use only one text. You may also want to differentiate by assigning different texts to different groups in the class.

Second, we have marked up and edited the informational text, highlighting key moments in the reading (and eliminating extraneous or distracting information).

Third, we have created a sidebar for use in working through the informational text. The sidebars ask students to reflect on the essential question, on the introduction, and on key ideas. They ask students to put key concepts and phrases with difficult vocabulary into their own words. And they call students' attention to both text features and concepts in the reading. The sidebar, then, offers guidance, helping the students to "chunk" and negotiate what might otherwise be an overwhelming text.

The strategies we offer also will help you to teach explicitly how students might work through challenging texts. Scaffold and modify as is appropriate. Some groups of students may require more teacher-directed instruction. Other groups may be able to move quickly into group and/or independent work.

Eventually, your students should be able to build their own units—finding interesting informational texts; identifying key, challenging vocabulary words; creating their own sidebar questions; and even developing check-for-understanding questions. Imagine a class full of students who can take ownership of their learning!

Regardless of whether your students approach this level of skill at the end of the school year or whether they achieve it by October, the strategies we offer throughout the units will allow you to build students' skills and confidence in reading challenging texts and in making critical cross-text connections.

PHOTOCOPYING
We have secured reproduction permission so that you can copy these articles for use with your students. Encourage your students to mark up and annotate the copies as they read.

DISCUSSION AND WRITING PROMPTS

For each article, we have created a range of discussion and writing activities. Each begins with discussion questions that can be used as do-nows, in small-group or whole-class discussion, or as homework. Feel free as well to use some of these discussion questions as classroom activities without asking your students to complete the follow-up writing task.

Also, we have created graphic organizers to help students prepare to write by assembling and organizing their evidence. In general, the organizers include examples to model for students how to go about collecting and discussing textual evidence. The organizers can be downloaded from www.usinginformationaltext.com/student, and you can modify them as necessary, particularly as you differentiate your instruction.

Each organizer is posted individually on the Student Resources page of our website: www.usinginformationaltext.com/student. If you have a class website where you post assignments, you can send students directly to any organizer you have assigned by linking directly to that file.

You can vary the expectations of the length of student responses for each writing task. We imagine an average length of one to two pages, although some prompts obviously lend themselves to longer responses. With each writing task, we explicitly call for the use of textual evidence to meet the emphasis on using evidence in the Writing Standard.

RUBRICS

For the writing prompts, we offer a suggested rubric that can be found at the end of the volume. Rubrics for the class activities (discussed below) are highly specific and are included at the end of the unit. All of our rubrics are also available at www.usinginformationaltext.com/teacher in formats that you can download and modify. The password to open the rubric files is gatsby18.

The rubrics help you communicate expectations to your students and incorporate the language and requirements of the CCSS. Feel free to adapt these rubrics to your own priorities and your students' needs. You also can develop your own grading criteria to correlate with the point structure of the rubric (e.g., 15–16 points = A-) or use the rubrics holistically. We encourage you to review the criteria on the rubric at the time you introduce the assignment, so that students are aware of your expectations. Rubrics also offer a valuable opportunity for the students to peer- and self-evaluate as they are revising.

CLASS ACTIVITIES

In addition to the writing and discussion activities, we have included a class-wide or small-group project that asks the students to produce more creative responses, addressing W3, "Write narratives to develop real or imagined experiences or events" (2010, 41); to work collaboratively (SL1, SL2, and SL3); and to present their knowledge and ideas (SL4, SL5, and SL6) in non-written or nonnarrative formats.

Some of the projects encourage the use of technology, addressing W6, "Use technology, including the Internet, to produce and publish writing and to interact and collaborate with others" (2010, 41), but they can be adapted easily depending on available resources.

These projects are often our favorite assignments because they ask students to apply their understanding of the informational text and the novel while tackling big ideas in projects that break the boundaries of the traditional essay. The projects develop diverse learning styles as well as students' abilities to use "strong content knowledge" and evidence to demonstrate not only comprehension but understanding of diverse perspectives, which the CCSS identifies as necessary for college and career readiness (2010, 7).

In order to forestall some of the difficulties of assessing creative and group projects, each class activity requires a narrative reflection, in which students must explain their goals and choices, and for group work, reflect on their group's collaborative process and their own role in the group.

These reflections give us much-needed information for assessment purposes, while also incorporating more traditional evidence-based writing into what is otherwise a nontraditional project. When the reflections ask students to reassess their own thinking and ideas after viewing or listening to their peers' presentations or performances, they also create an incentive for careful listening.

ANSWERS

Answers and sample responses to the questions in each unit are available on the series website: www.usinginformationaltext.com/teacher. The password to open the answer files is gatsby18. We provide an answer key, containing correct responses for all multiple-choice questions, as well as brief suggestions for the different constructed responses.

Our completed organizers and sample responses are not intended to serve as models for student use but to work as suggestive—by no means comprehensive—guidelines for teacher use. The responses are not the only correct answers; student responses should not be considered incorrect if they do not conform exactly.

STANDARDS

Our units address a range of CCSS, and we hope the inclusion of the relevant CCSS in the teacher's guide at the beginning of each unit is still useful to you, despite the fact that many states have moved into their own state-specific versions of the standards.

The vocabulary activities focus on knowledge of language (Anchor Standard L3) and vocabulary acquisition and use (Anchor Standards L4, L5, and L6). The use of key words also is reinforced in the writing activities and rubrics, so that students can use their vocabulary skills both "to comprehend complex texts and engage in purposeful writing about and conversations around content" (2010, 51).

The check-for-understanding questions for each unit reinforce the Language Standards for vocabulary while also integrating the Anchor Reading Standards: key ideas and details (RI1, RI2, and RI3), craft and structure (RI4, RI5, and RI6), and integration of knowledge and ideas (RI7, RI8, and RI9). All of the work of this volume is built around achieving RI10: building students' abilities to "Read and comprehend complex . . . informational texts independently and proficiently" (2010, 35). We pay particular attention in the reading sidebars and check-for-understanding questions to text features and structures because these elements of many informational texts are more challenging for many students.

Our discussion and writing questions build on the Language and Reading Standards and ask students to build competency in a wide variety of additional standards. Most units require students to synthesize multiple sources, meeting the Anchor Writing Standard, Research to Build and Present Knowledge (W7, W8, and W9). We ask students to "Write arguments to support claims in an analysis of substantive topics or texts" (W1) (2010, 41) or to "Write informative/explanatory texts to examine and convey complex ideas and information" (W2) (2010, 41).

WEBSITE AND BLOG

On our website (www.usinginformationaltext.org), we share updated teaching ideas. We hope you also will share feedback and ideas on our blog (usinginformationaltext.blogspot.com), email us at usinginfotext@gmail.com, or connect with us on Twitter (@usinginfotext).

CHOICE AND DURATION OF UNITS

Teachers often ask us how many units to include and how to choose. You do not need to use all of these units each time you teach *Gatsby*. Read through and choose those that will most enhance your approach to the text. We hope you will find one or more units helpful one year and decide to use others the next time around.

We are frequently asked how long each informational text unit should take in the classroom. There is no simple answer.

The work can be done quickly, when necessary. Groups of students can take on responsibility for different vocabulary exercises. And a fast-moving class can combine these exercises with the collective reading and discussion of a short informational text all in a forty-five-minute period.

But you may want to linger over an informational text, particularly to draw on that text for an in-depth writing assignment. If the curriculum dictates a short and shallow dive into one of the units, work briskly through one of the media clips, pass rapidly in groups through the vocabulary, and spend one or two class periods on the informational text.

Perhaps your students don't need the kind of testing review offered by the check-for-understanding questions, so skip those. And use the discussion and writing questions for in-class discussion only, offering the writing prompt only to students who need extra credit. This use of the informational text may then be completed in a few days of class.

Another group of students may necessitate a slower approach to the informational text unit; or you may decide that the connection is bearing significant fruit and you want to take more class time on the unit. In that case, you may spend class time reviewing the multiple-choice questions on the informational text, and in so doing help your students with their standardized test skills. You may take time talking through the discussion questions and working through the writing task for whichever assignment you or your students choose to take on.

If you choose a culminating class activity for the unit, you may find a broader audience for your students' presentation of their work. This may also require more class time, but the payoff will be worth the effort.

MAKE OUR MODEL YOUR OWN

Our volume makes the task of unearthing relevant context for *Gatsby* easier. We have worked to find and excerpt readable texts that fill in crucial gaps or pull out relevant connections, so teachers can meet the informational text standard in spaces of deep intellectual learning.

So, please, use our texts, but make them your own. Think about how many of the vocabulary activities you want to use. Or have your students make up their own. Would your students rather make up their own scenarios for the vocabulary skits? Let them go for it! Use our writing prompts for discussion only. Or skip right to the class activity.

We are offering one set of resources. Other possibilities abound. We hope our work will lighten the heavy load of teaching language arts today.

We also hope, however, that teachers will be inspired by the fascinating texts we have found; use our work as a model and find other connections that are particularly pertinent to your students. The one caution we want to offer, however, is that finding a great informational text is not the only work a teacher has to do in order to help her students find success with that text. Students need guidance in grappling with the challenges of informational text, and if you want more guidance on how to do this work, beyond following the model in this volume on *Gatsby*, we hope you will review our suggestions in *Connecting Across Disciplines: Collaborating with Informational Text*.

We are strong advocates of teacher-created materials. In fact, one of the exciting possibilities of the Informational Text Standard is the autonomy it restores to the teacher. The standard asks teachers to be curriculum creators, actively pulling material into the classroom that will meet the needs of her students.

When teachers supplement their teaching of literary standards with a vast array of text types, including new, timely texts as well as classics such as the seminal U.S. documents specifically named in the Common Core (and the kinds of nonliterary texts we are seeing on the PARCC and Smarter Balanced assessments), they create an atmosphere of active learning and make their classrooms labs for the development of skilled readers and thinkers. All teachers strive to do this; after all, this is why we went into the teaching profession—we love learning and want to instill that love of learning in our students.

CROSS-DISCIPLINARY COLLABORATION

We also want to encourage you to collaborate with your content area colleagues. Literacy is everyone's responsibility, but our non-language arts peers need our help. Collaborating on cross-disciplinary material such as Supreme Court cases, other historically significant documents, or social science research that connects with *Gatsby* can be the start of fruitful cross-disciplinary connections. Even the math teachers can help your students work with the data and graphs in some of our included readings. We have tried to highlight opportunities for these kinds of collaboration, and we encourage you to reach out to your non-language arts teachers, using our model to support this work.

REFERENCES

Beck, Isabel L., Margaret G. McKeown, and Linda Kucan. 2002. *Bringing Words to Life*. New York: Guilford.

Common Core State Standards Initiative. 2010. *Common Core State Standards for English Language Arts and Literacy in History/Social Studies, Science, and Technical Subjects*. Washington, DC: Common Core State Standards Initiative.

Moffett, James, and Betty J. Wagner. 1991. *Student-Centered Language Arts, K–12*. New York: Heinemann.

Wiggins, Grant, and Jay McTighe. 2005. *Understanding by Design*. Upper Saddle River, NJ: Pearson.

NOTE

1. Modified from Wiggins and McTighe (2005, 110).

UNIT 1

Why Should We Care about Economic Inequality?

TEACHER'S GUIDE

Overview

Gatsby is set in the Roaring Twenties, a period of tremendous economic inequality. Many economists today think the American economy of the 2010s closely resembles that period. The rich are rich and growing richer. The poor and the middle-class have both less income and less wealth. The deck, according to some economists, is stacked against most Americans and "rigged" in favor of the super-wealthy. Even more troubling, research indicates that economic inequality may have long-term effects: income inequality is correlated with decreased socioeconomic mobility for children born to poor families.

In this section, we include two generally accessible discussions of economic research. The first, by Berkeley economics professors Emmanuel Saez and Gabriel Zucman, explains their research on the growing wealth gap, highlighting periods of relative economic equality and inequality in the United States. The second, by Obama White House Chief of Staff David Vandivier, explores economist Alan Krueger's idea of The Great Gatsby Curve, an illustration of the association between family wealth and economic mobility.

The readings in this section will help students understand the structural inequalities embedded in the 1920s society depicted in *Gatsby*: the advantages Tom Buchanan is born into and that James Gatz struggles to overcome. These readings can also help to underscore the relevance of these economic issues from the 1920s to fundamental, timeless questions of fairness and equity in the United States. Indeed, the question of whether the American Dream is equally accessible to all is at the heart of *Gatsby*, and, of course, is one that spans generational, political, economic, and social divides.

Timing

These excerpts do not connect in any direct way to any particular moment in *Gatsby*, so teachers can use them at any time, before, during, or after the reading of the novel, to allow students to think broadly about issues of economic fairness and inequality.

Consider the following guidelines regarding when to undertake the different activities:

Essential Question for Discussion and Writing	Objective	Suggested Timing	Additional Research
A. How far apart are the haves and the have-nots in the United States? RI 1, 2, 3, 4, 5, 6, 7, 8, 9, 10 W 1, 2, 4, 5, 9, 10 SL 1, 4 L 1, 2, 3, 5, 6	Students will (SW) analyze economic research comparing wealth inequality today with the 1920s and a policy blog exploring the relationship between inequality and economic mobility in different nations in order to write an essay exploring whether the United States is the land of opportunity where a poor child can work hard and achieve great success.	Any time—this set of questions doesn't require any knowledge of *Gatsby*.	N
B. Does wealth make all the difference in *Gatsby*? RL 1, 2, 3, 4, 10 RI 1, 2, 3, 4, 5, 6, 7, 8, 9, 10 W 1, 2, 4, 5, 9, 10 SL 1, 4 L 1, 2, 3, 5, 6	SW use "What Is The Great Gatsby Curve" to consider the advantages and disadvantages of income in order to write an essay exploring the difference wealth makes in *Gatsby*.	Any time or after chapter 1 (when we learn about Tom's and Nick's backgrounds) and/or after chapter 6 (when we learn about Gatsby's)	N

Essential Question for Discussion and Writing	Objective	Suggested Timing	Additional Research
C. Is Gatsby a victim of The Great Gatsby Curve? RL 1, 2, 3, 4, 5, 10 RI 1, 2, 3, 4, 5, 6, 7, 8, 9, 10 W 1, 2, 4, 5, 7, 8, 9, 10 SL 1, 4 L 1, 2, 3, 5, 6	SW use "What Is The Great Gatsby Curve" and basic research about robber barons to think about the contrast between inherited wealth and Gatsby's attempts to make money and move up the economic ladder in order to write an essay considering whether Gatsby reflects the accuracy or inaccuracy of The Great Gatsby Curve.	After chapter 6 (when we learn about how Gatsby has made his money) or after chapter 8 (when Gatsby's fall is completed by his death)	Y
Class Activities			
Write a new scene for the novel from the perspective of one of the minor, less-privileged characters, reflecting a different perspective on any of the events of the text. RL 1, 2, 3, 4, 5, 6, 10 RI 1, 2, 3, 4, 5, 6, 7, 8, 9, 10 W 1, 2, 3, 4, 5, 9, 10 SL 1, 4 L 1, 2, 3, 5, 6	SW use their understanding of economic inequality and the difficulty of economic mobility to write a new scene for the novel illustrating the different perspective of a minor, less-privileged character.	If students are given full choice of which character they select, this activity needs to be completed after they have finished the novel; alternatively, this activity might be implemented for any one particular character after reading his or her section of the novel.	N
Prepare testimony and engage in a White House meeting about issues of inequality and then write a presidential address on the issues. RL 1, 2, 3, 4, 5, 10 RI 1, 2, 3, 4, 5, 6, 7, 8, 9, 10 W 1, 2, 4, 5, 9, 10 SL 1, 4 L 1, 2, 3, 5, 6	Focusing on the issues on inequality in the informational readings and *Gatsby*, SW prepare testimony, present a White House meeting (either in class or previously recorded), reflect on that meeting, and write a presidential address on the issues.	After finishing the novel	N

A suggested rubric for the writing prompts is available at the end of the volume and on our website, www.usinginformationaltext.com/teacher. The class activity rubric is included at the end of the unit and also on our website.

NOTES ON THE READINGS

- The graphs in the two readings are important and potentially challenging. Teachers will want to work carefully with students on how to read these graphs and how they serve the larger claims of the readings. We offer some exercises in the Writing and Discussion section for helping students work through the visual representations of data. The graphs also offer an opportunity to collaborate with your peer math teacher, particularly in terms of helping students to understand the different scales used in the graphs and think about why the authors chose to represent the data in this way. This kind of cross-disciplinary collaboration can help students be active and critical in their analysis of data, helping them to think through representations of data as claims that the authors are making (rather than simply as representations of unquestionable facts).
- It's worth underscoring with students that the focus here is on *degrees* of wealth with which *nearly all* will be unfamiliar. Saez and Gabriel are particularly interested in the economic inequality represented by the super ultra-wealthy: "The top 0.1 percent includes 160,000 families with total net assets of more than $20 million in 2012."
- Some of the references in *Gatsby* to the world and privilege of the wealthy are somewhat coded and potentially unfamiliar—the polo ponies and the Senior Society at what would have then been an entirely exclusive world at Yale University. Other references to wealth and excess within the novel are more obvious.
- Our volume on *A Raisin in the Sun* includes a unit focused on whether America is the land of opportunity. Our reading for that unit is Raj Chetty et al.'s "Where is the Land of Opportunity?," focused on variations of economic mobility within different geographic areas of the United States. Our excerpt of Chetty's research study in our *Raisin* volume would complement this unit's focus on economic inequality and social mobility in *Gatsby*.

SUGGESTED MEDIA LINKS

- Nicholas Kristof's "America's Stacked Deck" in the *New York Times* (February 18, 2016) builds on some of the economic research in this unit in order to think about what he calls "the antiestablishment campaigns" of Donald Trump and Bernie Sanders.

- The scholars involved in the Raj Chetty study mentioned above created a website, The Equality of Opportunity Project, that contains a wealth of additional information. Teachers may also want to use short clips from the video presentations about the study made by Raj Chetty to the World Bank and the British Academy. A comprehensive ranking of social mobility by U.S. city is also included on the website.
- The *New York Times* has created an interactive map displaying, in color, the differences across areas of the country in absolute upward mobility of children who grow up in below-median income families. Students can look up statistics for their own area, compare areas of their own choosing, and study regional trends in upward mobility. The map can be found on the *New York Times* website, as part of a feature called "In Climbing Income Ladder, Location Matters."
- A short YouTube video called "The Racial Wealth Gap in America," produced and based on research by the Urban Institute, uses snazzy but super-fast graphics to review the wealth gap in America. This video lays out the issues quickly; students likely will need multiple viewings to take in all of the information presented.
- The trailer for former secretary of labor Robert Reich's *Inequality for All* documentary, available on YouTube, is a quick and easy distillation of the issues of economic inequality in this unit and also offers a nice, brief discussion of The Great Prosperity, from 1947 to 1977, when the United States had much lower rates of economic inequality.
- "Wealth Inequality in America, Perception vs. Reality," a YouTube video produced by Crisis Forums, offers some quick, effective visuals about the differences between what Americans think wealth distribution in the United States should be, what Americans think wealth distribution is, and the reality of wealth distribution. The combination of narration and graphics will certainly help students acclimate to the graphic information presented in the readings in this unit.
- The Pew Charitable Trusts offers a brief, useful three-minute video, "Economic Mobility and the American Dream," on the difference between absolute and relative mobility in relation to the issue of economic mobility in the United States.
- A plethora of political cartoons on the subject of income inequality can serve to delight your students and stir an initial discussion of the issues. Find these through a search of Google Images.

VOCABULARY WARM-UP

WORDS TO OWN: assets, bubble, democratization, disparity, dystopia, erosion, evolution, exacerbated, inverted, jeopardize, meritocracy, projections, provocative, prudent, stock

Section A: Use context clues: Read the following sentences and use context clues to determine the meaning of the italicized words.

1. Saez and Zucman write that from the 1930s through the 1970s, there was a "*democratization* of wealth." If democracy theoretically gives all people access to a vote and therefore a voice in government, what do you think it might mean for wealth to be *democratized*? Would more or fewer people have wealth? Do you think a *democratization* of wealth would mean total wealth equality? Do we have total political equality in our democracy?

2. My doctor says that if I drink a lot of caffeine before an exam I will *exacerbate* my nervousness. I disagree; although exams already make me anxious, I think caffeine can energize me without making me jumpy. What *exacerbates* your anxieties? What calms your anxieties? Why?

3. I encourage my students to be *provocative* in their editorials for the student newspaper, but they also need to realize that other teachers and administrators may not agree with or may even take offense at their *provocative* opinions. What *provocative* ideas or images do you think are inappropriate in a student newspaper? What *provocative* ideas or images do you think belong in a student newspaper? What do you think is the purpose of trying to be *provocative*?

4. If a democracy is a system built around the *demos*, the people, then a *meritocracy* would be a system built around what? Do you think the United States is a *meritocracy*? Can we separately measure someone's merit and value without taking the advantages of background, culture, and class into account? Do you think we should try?

May be photocopied for classroom use. *Using Informational Text to Teach* The Great Gatsby by Audrey Fisch and Susan Chenelle © 2018 (Lanham, MD: Rowman & Littlefield).

5. If you break the rules by bringing food into the computer lab, you *jeopardize* your chances of being allowed to go on the field trip. But perhaps you won't get caught, and then you'll still be able to go on the trip. Is it worth the risk? How do you decide whether something is worth putting yourself into a position of *jeopardy*? When is *jeopardizing* your future not worth a short-term reward or pleasure?

6. In political campaigns, some candidates offer small, careful, *prudent* solutions and others offer grand, unreasonable, or impractical suggestions. Given that we have big problems that we need to address, do you prefer the *prudent* or the radical candidate? Is the *prudent* choice always the best one? Do you prefer a bigger risk for a bigger reward?

Section B: More context clues: Here your task is to use context clues to understand the italicized word's meaning AND to practice your context clues skills.

1. "Wealth is the stock of all the *assets* people own, including their homes, pension saving, and bank accounts, minus all debt." *Assets* can best be defined as

    a) money
    b) financial resources
    c) savings
    d) accounting

2. Which word(s) from the sentence in Question 1 best helps the reader understand the meaning of *assets*?

    a) minus all debt
    b) pension
    c) including their homes, pension saving, and bank accounts
    d) people

3. Saez and Zucman write about how average wealth for 90 percent of families has stayed the same while it has more than tripled for a small group of very wealthy families. The writers then ask, "How can we explain the growing disparity in American wealth?" What is another way of asking their question?

   a) Why are some more and more wealthy when the wealth of most families has remained the same?
   b) Why is there more wealth in America and less in other countries?
   c) Why are the rich richer and the poor poorer?
   d) How did the very wealthy triple their wealth?

4. What information in Question 3 best helps you understand what the authors are trying to understand about a *disparity* in American wealth?

   a) average wealth for 90 percent of families has stayed the same
   b) it has more than tripled for a small group of very wealthy families
   c) a and b
   d) neither a nor b

5. Vandivier explains, "According to *projections*, 'the advantages and disadvantages of income passed from parents to the children is predicted to rise.'" By *projections*, Vandivier means

   a) facts
   b) government plans
   c) random guesses
   d) research-based hypotheses

6. Which word(s) from the sentences in Question 5 best help you understand the meaning of *projections*?

   a) advantages
   b) predicted
   c) According to
   d) to rise

Section C: Sometimes common words are used in uncommon ways. **Use the dictionary** in order to understand the uncommon meanings of the italicized common words.

1. Saez and Zucman write, "Wealth is the *stock* of all the assets people own, including their homes, pension saving, and bank accounts." By *stock* here Saez and Zucman can't mean shares in a company because they also mention homes, pension saving, and bank accounts, which are not shares in a company. What other definition of *stock* are they using?

2. Saez and Zucman describe the "*evolution* of wealth inequality." What does this mean, in your own words? How and why do you think inequality might *evolve*? Do you think the *evolution* of inequality is necessarily a good or a bad thing? Is *evolution* generally good or bad, in your opinion?

3. Saez and Zucman are interested in the "*erosion* of wealth among the middle class and the poor." Have you studied the effects of soil *erosion*? What happens to a riverbank when soil *erodes*? If wealth is *eroding* for some people in our country, what does that mean? What could be the consequences of the *erosion* of wealth for our country overall?

4. Saez and Zucman describe two economic events: the stock-market *bubble* and the housing *bubble*. What does the term *bubble* suggest to you about these events? Before you look up the word, think about the qualities of a *bubble*. Then, check the dictionary definition. How does a housing *bubble* reflect the quality of the word *bubble*? What do you think happens to people and their financial health when a housing *bubble* bursts?

Section D: Use the dictionary to look up the italicized words and answer the following questions based on their definitions.

1. Thomas Piketty describes income inequality as a threat to American ideals, and the Berkeley economists cite his ideas to warn about a *dystopian* future. Do you worry about the United States becoming a *dystopia*? Do you think income inequality might play a role in turning our country into a *dystopia*? Why?

2. It was once considered ugly to be thin; body fat was considered a sign of privilege and wealth. That trend was then *inverted*, and now a slender physique is considered a marker of power and prestige. Why do you think this particular trend *inverted*? Can you think of any other trends that have similarly *inverted* over time? Do you expect any current trends to *invert* in the future?

3. Is there a *disparity* in the respect and admiration given to male and female athletes in your school? To what do you attribute this *disparity*? Do you think this *disparity* will change in the future?

4. There has been a great deal of discussion about bullying and social media. Do you think social media *exacerbates* bullying, or is bullying on social media just bullying in another form and place? What, beyond social media, do you think *exacerbates* bullying today?

5. Do you believe the United States is a *meritocracy*? Why or why not? What do you think are the key features of a true *meritocracy*?

6. What kind of a future do you *project* for yourself? On what experiences and evidence from your past do you form this *projection* for/of your future?

7. Do you think students should be allowed to be *provocative* in their dress and ideas? Should school be a place for edgy exploration? Explain why or why not.

8. How would you respond to a friend who is *jeopardizing* her future by engaging in risky or dangerous behavior? How would you decide whether or not to warn him or her?

Section E: Practice using the word correctly by choosing the correct form of the word(s) that best fits in the blank within the following sentences.

1. The United States is a nation of many ____; some think our many differences make us stronger as a nation, but inequality among our people is also a tremendous challenge.

   a) disparity
   b) disparate
   c) disparities
   d) disparates

2. I want to be ____ in how I approach the teacher; I'm worried that she doesn't like me, and it's really important that I do well in this class.

   a) prudish
   b) prude
   c) prudent
   d) prudes

3. It is difficult to build up goodwill among teachers, students, and administrators in a school; unfortunately, one negative event can easily ____ much of that goodwill.

   a) erosion
   b) erode
   c) eroded
   d) erodes

4. I have watched the political climate ____ over my lifetime, and I worry that productive political dialogue is being replaced with senseless political provocation.

   a) evolve
   b) evolution
   c) evolved
   d) evolves

Section F: Vocabulary skits
Use the model sentences and definitions to understand the words in question. Create a skit in which you address the given topic. Every member of the group must use the vocabulary word at least once during your performance of the skit.

1. *disparity*—inequality, difference

    - I abhor the *disparate* treatment of men and women by the media.
    - There should be no wage *disparity* between men and women: equal work for equal pay!
    - Scholars interested in education may want to focus their attention on the many *disparities* between public and private schools.

Scenario: Create a skit in which a group of aspiring actors discusses the *disparity* of opportunities available in Hollywood. Is there a wide range of roles available for actors, regardless of gender, race, and age? Are *disparities* in the kinds and number of roles available inevitable, given the demands of the market and audiences? How do these young actors feel about the *disparate* opportunities they face?

2. *democratization*—the process of making or becoming more democratic, more politically or socially equal

    - Do you think war is a practical way to *democratize* a country and spread equality?
    - *Democratization* is a difficult process; creating a world in which everyone has an equal voice is neither simple nor easy.
    - Some people feel that *democratization* in media has been dangerous; social media means that everyone can spread information, even those who don't really know what they are talking about.

Scenario: Recently, the music industry has undergone massive *democratization*. Instead of needing to seek the approval of music industry giants, a new artist can record his or her music and post it online, where millions of people around the world can access that music. Create a skit in which a group of young musicians discusses the *democratization* of the music industry. Do they all feel that this industry shift is a win-win for musicians? What are the downsides to the *democratization* of this field?

May be photocopied for classroom use. *Using Informational Text to Teach* The Great Gatsby by Audrey Fisch and Susan Chenelle © 2018 (Lanham, MD: Rowman & Littlefield).

3. *meritocracy*—a system in which merit, talent, and ability are rewarded, rather than wealth, background, or connections

- If the United States government were a *meritocracy*, we should have more female political leaders!
- My family does not function as a *meritocracy*; my brother gets all of the privileges, even though I do better in school.
- It is easy to celebrate the idea of a *meritocracy*, but it is difficult to decide what counts as *merit* and even more difficult to measure *merit*.

Scenario: Create a skit in which a group of students organizes a protest of the SAT, arguing that this test undermines *meritocracy* in education. The students might cite as evidence research that suggests that the SAT favors men over women, white test-takers over test-takers of color, wealthy test-takers over poor test-takers, and students with well-educated parents over students whose parents have not received traditional education. How do the students think *merit* in education should be measured? What pro-*meritocracy* and anti-SAT slogans might they create to use in their campaign?

4. *provocative*—serving to excite, irritate, provoke

- The slogan on her T-shirt was politically *provocative*, so the principal sent her home to change clothes.
- Why do you always have to be so *provocative*; can't you sit quietly and go along with everyone else sometimes?
- I wasn't trying to *provoke* the drama students, but someone needed to explain to them that casting a male as Juliet wasn't a *provocative* choice in the Elizabethan era.

Scenario: The theater club is considering the choice for the spring play. One play under consideration features a suicide, and some of the students feel that choice would be too *provocative*. Other students think the point of a play is to *provoke* thinking and discussion, particularly about an issue of importance to young people. Create a skit in which the students address the theater adviser and the school principal about the pros and cons of their choice.

ESSENTIAL QUESTION: WHY SHOULD WE CARE ABOUT ECONOMIC INEQUALITY?

Introduction to the Unit

> **Reflect on the essential question:** Why does economic inequality matter? Where do you see economic inequality in the world you live in? How does economic inequality affect you?

Economic inequality, the gap between rich and poor, reached a peak in the 1920s, and F. Scott Fitzgerald's *The Great Gatsby* has come to define the tragedy of the Roaring Twenties. Unfortunately, inequality is not a historical issue from the past; it has emerged recently as one of the defining problems of our time. Below, you will read two articles that discuss the impact of economic inequality today.

In the first, a blog post, two economics professors from the University of California at Berkeley discuss both income inequality (inequalities in wages) and wealth inequality (inequalities in overall assets, including savings and debt). They argue that high levels of income and wealth inequality threaten the core American value of equal opportunity for all. The second article, written by a staff member of the Council of Economic Advisors, explains the economic idea of The Great Gatsby Curve, a graphic representation of the relation between economic inequality and economic mobility. In areas of the world where income inequality is higher, children from poor families are less likely to be able to move out of poverty.

If, as the first article suggests, the United States has become a place of great inequality, what does this mean for the next generation? Will young people, regardless of their background, be able to work hard and get ahead? Reading these pieces together makes clear that inequality affects more than just one generation and threatens the American Dream.

> **Research and reflect on the introduction:** The introduction suggests that the economic inequality we are experiencing today parallels inequality Americans experienced in the 1920s. How did the Roaring Twenties end? What might we learn from this past? What possible outcomes do you see for our current climate of inequality? What do you hope might happen? What do you fear?

May be photocopied for classroom use. *Using Informational Text to Teach* The Great Gatsby by Audrey Fisch and Susan Chenelle © 2018 (Lanham, MD: Rowman & Littlefield).

READING #1: EXCERPT FROM A BLOG POST PUBLISHED BY A RESEARCH ORGANIZATION FOCUSED ON THE U.S. ECONOMY

Introduction

Below is a piece written by two economics professors for the website of a research organization focused on the U.S. economy. They argue that economic inequality decreased from the 1930s through the 1970s but has since exploded. They compare recent levels of wealth inequality to conditions in the Roaring Twenties and worry about a dystopian future of haves and have-nots in which American ideals of opportunity are threatened. The issue of opportunity, raised by Saez and Zucman here, is taken up more fully in reading #2.

> **Reflect** on the kind of piece you are reading. What is the purpose of the piece? Who do you think is the intended audience? How reliable do you think the information presented is? What can you tell about the research organization for which they write? How is this kind of research and writing different from journalism you might read in a newspaper?
>
> **Reflect on the title:** How does the language choice in the title reflect the authors' point of view on their subject? Why do you think they selected such a provocative title?

From "Exploding wealth inequality in the United States" by Emmanuel Saez and Gabriel Zucman

There is no dispute that income inequality has been on the rise in the United States for the past four decades. The share of total income earned by the top 1 percent of families was less than 10 percent in the late 1970s but now exceeds 20 percent as of the end of 2012. A large portion of this increase is due to an upsurge in the labor incomes earned by senior company executives and successful entrepreneurs. But is the rise in U.S. economic inequality purely a matter of rising labor compensation at the top, or did wealth inequality rise as well?

Before we answer that question (hint: the answer is a definitive yes, as we will demonstrate below) we need to define what we mean by wealth. Wealth is the *stock* of all the *assets* people own, including their homes, pension saving, and bank accounts, minus all debts. Wealth can be self-made out of work and saving, but it can also be inherited . . .

> **Key idea:** Think about the distinction between income inequality and wealth inequality. What do Saez and Zucman mean when they say that wealth can be "self-made out of work and saving, but it can also be inherited"? Why is inherited wealth not self-made?

May be photocopied for classroom use. *Using Informational Text to Teach* The Great Gatsby by Audrey Fisch and Susan Chenelle © 2018 (Lanham, MD: Rowman & Littlefield). Excerpts from "Exploding wealth inequality in the United States" by Emmanuel Saez and Gabriel Zucman. Equitable Growth. Reprinted by permission of the authors. All rights reserved.

Wealth inequality, it turns out, has followed a spectacular U-shape *evolution* over the past one hundred years. From the Great Depression in the 1930s through the late 1970s there was a substantial *democratization* of wealth. The trend then *inverted*, with the share of total household wealth owned by the top 0.1 percent increasing to 22 percent in 2012 from 7 percent in the late 1970s. (See Figure 1.1.) The top 0.1 percent includes 160,000 families with total net *assets* of more than $20 million in 2012.

Figure 1.1 shows that wealth inequality has exploded in the United States over the past four decades. The share of wealth held by the top 0.1 percent of families is now almost as high as in the late 1920s, when *The Great Gatsby* defined an era that rested on the inherited fortunes of the robber barons of the Gilded Age.

In recent decades, only a tiny fraction of the population saw its wealth share grow. While the

> **Vocabulary:** Saez and Zucman note a "substantial democratization of wealth." Put this into your own words. What does it mean for wealth to be democratized? Do you think this is a good thing?
>
> **Reflect:** The top 0.1 percent owned 7 percent of total household wealth in the late 1970s and then 22 percent of total household wealth in 2012. What does this mean? Did the wealthiest families, the top 0.1 percent, own a smaller or larger share of the total wealth of the country in 2012 than in 1974? Why do you think this might matter?

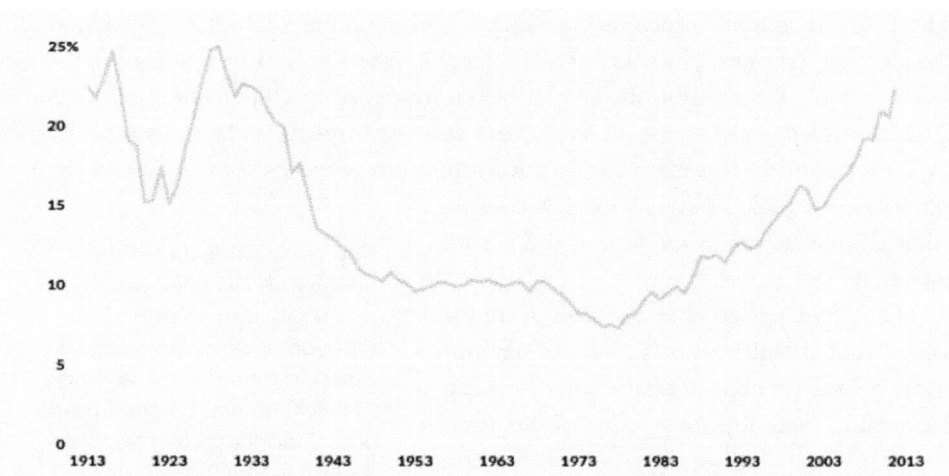

Figure 1.1 The Return of the Roaring Twenties. The share of total U.S. wealth owned by the top 0.1 percent of families, 1913–2012.

May be photocopied for classroom use. *Using Informational Text to Teach* The Great Gatsby by Audrey Fisch and Susan Chenelle © 2018 (Lanham, MD: Rowman & Littlefield). Excerpts from "Exploding wealth inequality in the United States" by Emmanuel Saez and Gabriel Zucman. Equitable Growth. Reprinted by permission of the authors. All rights reserved.

WHY SHOULD WE CARE ABOUT ECONOMIC INEQUALITY? 17

wealth share of the top 0.1 percent increased a lot in recent decades, that of the next 0.9 percent (families between the top 1 percent and the top 0.1 percent) did not. . . . In other words, family fortunes of $20 million or more grew much faster than those of only a few millions.

The flip side of these trends at the top of the wealth ladder is the *erosion* of wealth among the middle class and the poor. There is a widespread public view across American society that a key structural change in the U.S. economy since the 1920s is the rise of middle-class wealth, in particular because of the development of pensions and the rise in home ownership rates. But our results show that while the share of wealth of the bottom 90 percent of families did gradually increase from 15 percent in the 1920s to a peak of 36 percent in the mid-1980s, it then dramatically declined. By 2012, the bottom 90 percent collectively owned only 23 percent of total U.S. wealth, about as much as in 1940. (See Figure 1.2.)

> **Reflect on the caption of the graph in Figure 1.1:** How and why does the graph indicate the return of the Roaring Twenties? What quality of wealth defined the Roaring Twenties and how and when is that quality reflected in the graph?
>
> **Key idea:** Why do Saez and Zucman distinguish between the wealth share of the top 0.1 percent and the next 0.9 percent? Aren't they all super wealthy? What point are the writers making here?

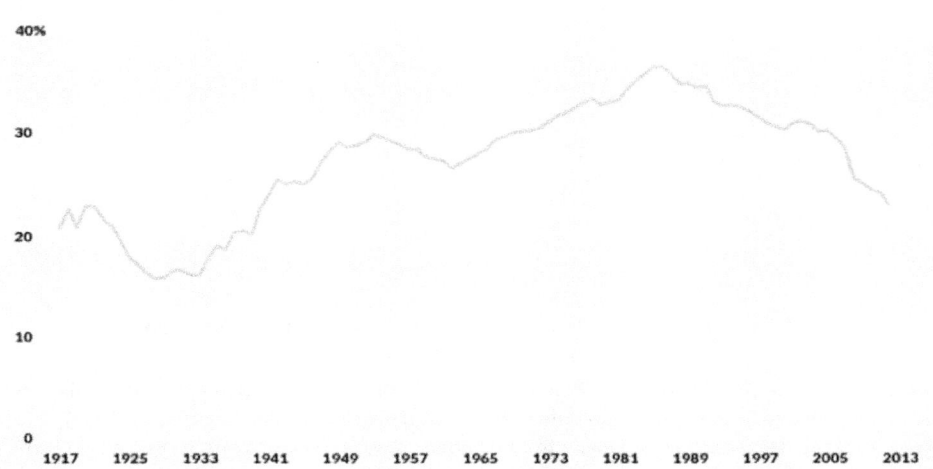

Figure 1.2 The Rise and Fall of Middle-Class Wealth. The share of total U.S. wealth owned by the bottom 90 percent of families, 1917–2012.

May be photocopied for classroom use. *Using Informational Text to Teach* The Great Gatsby by Audrey Fisch and Susan Chenelle © 2018 (Lanham, MD: Rowman & Littlefield). Excerpts from "Exploding wealth inequality in the United States" by Emmanuel Saez and Gabriel Zucman. Equitable Growth. Reprinted by permission of the authors. All rights reserved.

The growing indebtedness of most Americans is the main reason behind the *erosion* of the wealth share of the bottom 90 percent of families. Many middle-class families own homes and have pensions, but too many of these families also have much higher mortgages to repay and much higher consumer credit and student loans to service than before. For a time, rising indebtedness was compensated by the increase in the market value of the *assets* of middle-class families. The average wealth of the bottom 90 percent of families jumped during the stock-market *bubble* of the late 1990s and the housing *bubble* of the early 2000s. But it then collapsed during and after the Great Recession of 2007–2009. (See Figure 1.3.)

Reflect on the caption of the graph in Figure 1.2: Why is the wealth of the bottom 90 percent of families important? At which two times was the percentage of this wealth the least? What does this graph then indicate about the level of wealth inequality in these two times?

Key idea: What, according to the authors, is the reason the wealth of the bottom 90 percent of families has fallen recently?

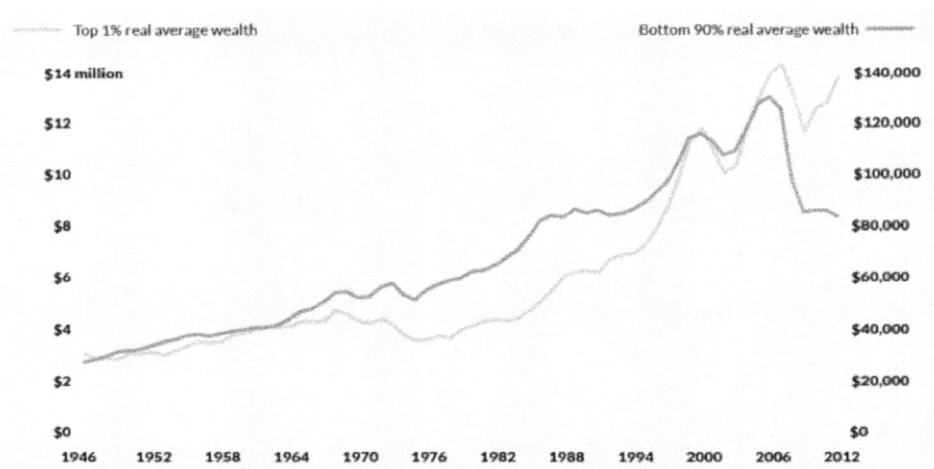

Figure 1.3 The New Wealth Divide in the United States. The average wealth of families in the bottom 90 percent and the top 1 percent of the wealth distribution, in constant 2010 U.S. dollars, 1946–2012. *Notes*: The figure depicts the average real wealth of bottom 90 percent of families (right y-axis) and top 1 percent families (left y-axis) from 1946 to 2012. The scales differ by a factor 100 to reflect the fact that top 1 percent of families are 100 times richer than the bottom 90 percent of families.

May be photocopied for classroom use. *Using Informational Text to Teach* The Great Gatsby by Audrey Fisch and Susan Chenelle © 2018 (Lanham, MD: Rowman & Littlefield). Excerpts from "Exploding wealth inequality in the United States" by Emmanuel Saez and Gabriel Zucman. Equitable Growth. Reprinted by permission of the authors. All rights reserved.

Since the housing and financial crises of the late 2000s, there has been no recovery in the wealth of the middle class and the poor. The average wealth of the bottom 90 percent of families is equal to $80,000 in 2012—the same level as in 1986. In contrast, the average wealth for the top 1 percent more than tripled between 1980 and 2012. In 2012, the wealth of the top 1 percent increased almost back to its peak level of 2007. The Great Recession looks only like a small bump along an upward trajectory.

How can we explain the growing *disparity* in American wealth? The answer is that the combination of higher income inequality alongside a growing *disparity* in the ability to save for most Americans is fueling the explosion in wealth inequality.

For the bottom 90 percent of families, real wage gains (after factoring in inflation) were very limited over the past three decades, but for their counterparts in the top 1 percent real wages grew fast. In addition, the saving rate of middle-class and lower-class families collapsed over the same period while it remained substantial at the top. Today, the top 1 percent of families save about 35 percent of their income, while the bottom 90 percent of families save about zero.

> **Reflect on the caption of the graph in Figure 1.3:** Why does the caption reference a divide? How is this divide reflected in the two lines in this graph? When was the wealth divide between the 1% and the 90% greatest? When was the divide smallest?
>
> **Reflect on the notes for the graph in Figure 1.3:** What does it mean that the scales on the left and right y-axes of the graph "differ by a factor of 100"? Why do you think the writers made this design choice for their graph? How does their design choice impact our understanding of the numbers and the issues?
>
> **Key idea:** What two ideas do Saez and Zucman offer to account for the disparity between the wealth of the 1% and of the 90%?

THE IMPLICATIONS OF RISING WEALTH INEQUALITY AND POSSIBLE REMEDIES

If income inequality stays high and if the saving rate of the bottom 90 percent of families remains low, then wealth *disparity* will keep increasing. . . . While the rich would be extremely rich, ordinary families would own next to nothing, with debts almost as high

> **Reflect on the heading:** Why do you think Saez and Zucman use this heading here? How does this section of their writing differ from what they offer above?

May be photocopied for classroom use. *Using Informational Text to Teach* The Great Gatsby by Audrey Fisch and Susan Chenelle © 2018 (Lanham, MD: Rowman & Littlefield). Excerpts from "Exploding wealth inequality in the United States" by Emmanuel Saez and Gabriel Zucman. Equitable Growth. Reprinted by permission of the authors. All rights reserved.

as their *assets*. Paris School of Economics professor Thomas Piketty warns that inherited wealth could become the defining line between the haves and the have-nots in the 21st century. This *provocative* prediction hit a nerve in the United States this year when Piketty's book *Capital in the 21st Century* became a national best seller because it outlined a direct threat to the cherished American ideals of *meritocracy* and opportunity.

What should be done to avoid this *dystopian* future? We need policies that reduce the concentration of wealth, prevent the transformation of self-made wealth into inherited fortunes, and encourage savings among the middle class. There are a number of specific policy reforms needed to rebuild middle-class wealth. A combination of *prudent* financial regulation to rein in predatory lending, incentives to help people save—nudges have been shown to be very effective in the case of 401(k) pensions—and more generally steps to boost the wages of the bottom 90 percent of workers are needed so that ordinary families can afford to save.

> **Key idea:** Why, according to Thomas Piketty, might income inequality be a threat to American ideals? Do you think Saez and Zucman agree with Piketty's assessment of the dangers of income inequality? What do you think?
>
> **Vocabulary:** What exactly do Saez and Zucman see here as the dystopian future? Why do they see this future as dystopian?

Saez, Emmanuel and Gabriel Zucman. "Exploding wealth inequality in the United States." *Equitablog*, The Washington Center for Equitable Growth, October 20, 2014, http://equitablegrowth.org/human-capital/exploding-wealth-inequality-united-states/.

May be photocopied for classroom use. *Using Informational Text to Teach* The Great Gatsby by Audrey Fisch and Susan Chenelle © 2018 (Lanham, MD: Rowman & Littlefield). Excerpts from "Exploding wealth inequality in the United States" by Emmanuel Saez and Gabriel Zucman. Equitable Growth. Reprinted by permission of the authors. All rights reserved.

READING #2: EXCERPT FROM A BLOG POST WRITTEN BY THE WHITE HOUSE CHIEF OF STAFF FOR THE COUNCIL OF ECONOMIC ADVISORS

Introduction

Below is an excerpt from David Vandivier, writing as part of his job as chief of staff for the Obama administration's Council of Economic Advisors. Below, Vandivier explains economist Alan Krueger's idea of The Great Gatsby Curve, an illustration of the relationship between family wealth and economic mobility across different nations. Read the text below and then analyze the figures that follow.

From "What Is The Great Gatsby Curve?" by David Vandivier

The Great Gatsby. You've probably heard of it—a novel by F. Scott Fitzgerald and now a movie (again) that highlights the inequality and class distinctions in America during the Roaring 20s.

But, unless you're an economist, you've likely never heard of The Great Gatsby Curve, introduced in a speech . . . by Alan Krueger, Chairman of the Council of Economic Advisors.

So what is it, then? As Chairman Krueger explained in his speech, The Great Gatsby Curve illustrates the connection between concentration of wealth in one generation and the ability of those in the next generation to move up the economic ladder compared to their parents.

Reflect on the introduction: What do you think it means to be chief of staff for the Council of Economic Advisors? What do you think David Vandivier's role is? What do you think his purpose is in writing a blog explaining an economist's ideas? Who do you think is the audience for this post?

Notice that the piece begins with a reference to *The Great Gatsby*. Why do you think Vandivier begins this way? Why do you think Krueger would have chosen to use Fitzgerald's novel to name his economic research?

Key idea: The curve focuses on the ability of children from poor families to improve economically as adults. Why would researchers care about economic mobility for poor children? What relationship does The Great Gatsby Curve show between income inequality and economic mobility?

Key idea: What is the Great Recession? (Check Wikipedia, if necessary.) What key economic point is Vandivier making about the Great Recession?

The curve shows that children from poor families are less likely to improve their economic status as adults in countries where income inequality was higher—meaning wealth was concentrated in fewer hands—around the time those children were growing up.

So why does this matter for the United States? The U.S. has had a sharp rise in inequality since the 1980s. In fact, on the eve of the Great Recession, income inequality in the U.S. was as sharp as it had been at any period since the time of *The Great Gatsby*.

"While we will not know for sure whether, and how much, income mobility across generations has been *exacerbated* by the rise in inequality in the U.S. until today's children have grown up and completed their careers," he said, "we can use The Great Gatsby Curve to make a rough forecast."

According to *projections*, "the advantages and disadvantages of income passed from parents to the children is predicted to rise by about a quarter for the next generation as a result of the rise in inequality that the U.S. has seen in the last 25 years," he said.

It is hard to look at these figures and not be concerned that rising inequality is *jeopardizing* our tradition of equality of opportunity. The fortunes of one's parents seem to matter increasingly in American society.

Vandivier, David. "What is The Great Gatsby Curve?" *Whitehouse.gov*, The White House, 11 June 2013, https://obamawhitehouse.archives.gov/blog/2013/06/11/what-great-gatsby-curve.

Vocabulary: Vandivier uses the word "exacerbated" to describe the possible effect of increased inequality on income mobility. So, does he mean that income mobility might get better or worse? If it is exacerbated, would that mean more income mobility or less income mobility?

Reflect: Vandivier claims that we won't know whether income mobility has been exacerbated by inequality until today's children have grown up. Put this point into your own words. Why won't we know the effect of income equality on these children until they grow up? What prediction do you think Vandivier might make about the income mobility of these poor children, based on The Great Gatsby Curve?

Key idea: What connection is Vandivier making between rising inequality and equality of opportunity? In your own words, explain his thinking.

Key idea: Why, according to Vandivier and The Great Gatsby Curve, do the fortunes of one's parents matter increasingly today? What do you think about this idea? Does this sentiment seem in keeping with typical American ideals of fairness and equality?

WHY SHOULD WE CARE ABOUT ECONOMIC INEQUALITY?

Analyze the following figures: On the horizontal line of the graphs (the X axis), the figures represent income distribution. What does income distribution mean? Which country has the greatest rate of income distribution?

Along the vertical line of the graphs (the Y axis), the figures represent economic mobility. A higher number along the axis of economic mobility translates into what outcome for a child?

New Zealand is in the middle of the graphs. What does this mean? How evenly is income distributed in New Zealand? How does economic mobility in New Zealand compare with Japan or Germany?

What argument do the two figures make about the relationship between income distribution and economic mobility? Where does the United States fit into that argument?

Figure 1.5 makes a projection about mobility. What is that projection? How is that projection built around the data presented?

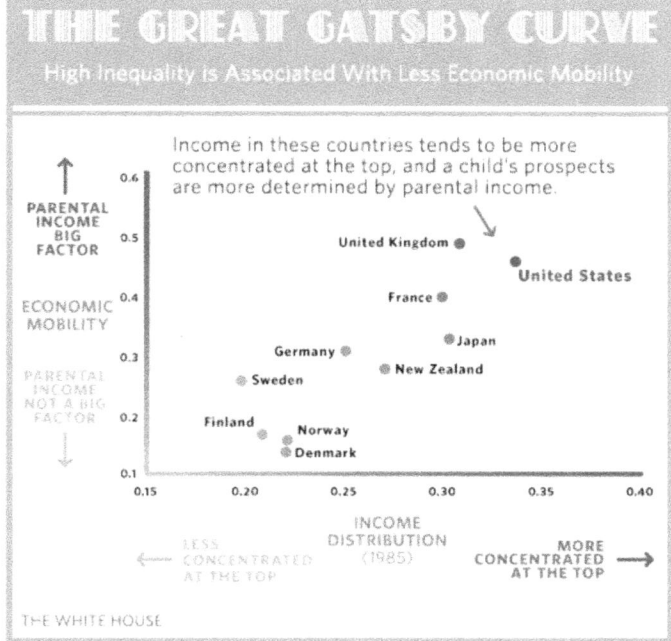

Figure 1.4 Income in These Countries Tends to Be More Concentrated at the Top

---

May be photocopied for classroom use. *Using Informational Text to Teach* The Great Gatsby by Audrey Fisch and Susan Chenelle © 2018 (Lanham, MD: Rowman & Littlefield).

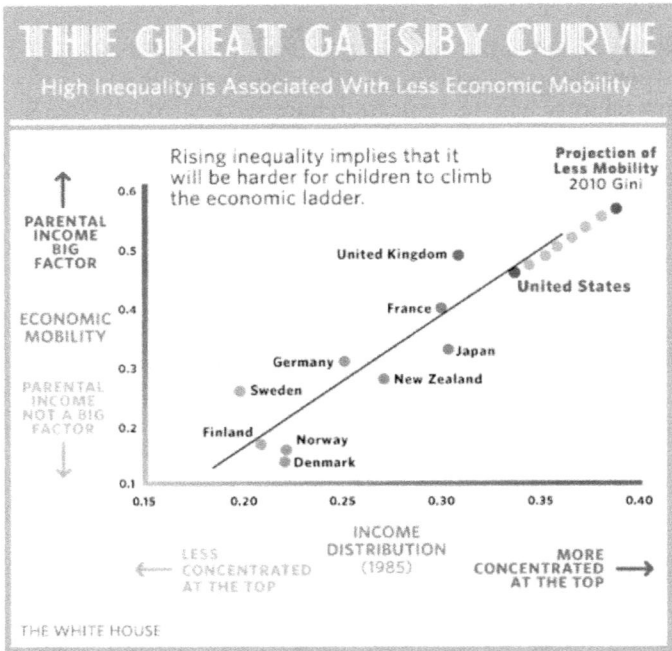

Figure 1.5 Rising Inequality Implies That It Will Be Harder for Children to Climb the Economic Ladder

CHECK FOR UNDERSTANDING

1. In what years was the share of total wealth owned by the wealthiest families in the United States highest?

    a) Between 1913 and 1923
    b) Between 1963 and 1973
    c) Between 1923 and 1933
    d) Between 2003 and 2013

2. What is the central idea of Saez and Zucman's essay?

    a) Growing wealth inequality represents a threat to ordinary families.
    b) Irresponsible borrowing is the main source of debt in the United States.
    c) Wealth inequality is greater than it has ever been in the United States.
    d) Wealth inequality has increased steadily over the past four decades and now approaches levels of inequality last seen in the Roaring Twenties.

3. Which THREE sentences from the text best support the answer to the question above?

    a) "The growing indebtedness of most Americans is the main reason behind the erosion of the wealth share of the bottom 90 percent of families."
    b) "The top 0.1 percent includes 160,000 families with total net assets of more than $20 million in 2012."
    c) "Wealth inequality, it turns out, has followed a spectacular U-shape evolution over the past 100 years."
    d) "The share of wealth held by the top 0.1 percent of families is now almost as high as in the late 1920s, when *The Great Gatsby* defined an era that rested on the inherited fortunes of the robber barons of the Gilded Age."
    e) "For the bottom 90 percent of families, real wage gains (after factoring in inflation) were very limited over the past three decades, but for their counterparts in the top 1 percent real wages grew fast."
    f) "There are a number of specific policy reforms needed to rebuild middle-class wealth."
    g) "Paris School of Economics professor Thomas Piketty warns that inherited wealth could become the defining line between the haves and the have-nots in the 21st century."

4. Saez and Zucman offer the idea that "The growing indebtedness of most Americans is the main reason behind the erosion of the wealth share of the bottom 90 percent of families." Which paraphrase best explains the authors' thinking here?

   a) Most Americans have borrowed too much money.
   b) Most Americans are in debt.
   c) Most Americans are not wealthy.
   d) Most Americans are less wealthy because of greater amounts of debt.

5. Which additional phrase(s) from the text helps you to understand the answer to Question 4?

   a) "Many middle-class families own homes and have pensions"
   b) "many of these families also have much higher mortgages to repay and much higher consumer credit and student loans to service than before"
   c) "the ability of those in the next generation to move up the economic ladder compared to their parents"
   d) "The average wealth of the bottom 90 percent of families jumped during the stock-market bubble of the late 1990s and the housing bubble of the early 2000s"

6. Who introduced the idea of The Great Gatsby Curve?

   a) F. Scott Fitzgerald
   b) David Vandivier
   c) Alan Krueger
   d) Thomas Piketty

7. Which question(s) is/are raised but not answered by The Great Gatsby Curve? More than one answer may be correct.

   a) How much income mobility will today's children have?
   b) Why does greater income inequality translate into smaller economic mobility?
   c) Why is the United States considered the land of equality and opportunity?
   d) Has inequality increased in the United States?

May be photocopied for classroom use. *Using Informational Text to Teach* The Great Gatsby by Audrey Fisch and Susan Chenelle © 2018 (Lanham, MD: Rowman & Littlefield).

8. Vandivier writes that "The fortunes of one's parents seem to matter increasingly in American society." What does he mean here by *fortunes*?

   a) luck
   b) wealth
   c) poverty
   d) prosperous

9. Which other two phrases from the article help to explain why the fortunes of one's parents increasingly matter in the United States?

   a) "the advantages and disadvantages of income passed from parents to the children"
   b) "The curve shows that children from poor families are less likely to improve their economic status as adults in countries where income inequality was higher"
   c) "The U.S. has had a sharp rise in inequality since the 1980s."
   d) "we can use The Great Gatsby Curve to make a rough forecast"

10. What is the purpose of the second sentence of the piece: "You've probably heard of it—a novel by F. Scott Fitzgerald and now a movie (again) that highlights the inequality and class distinctions in America during the Roaring 20s"?

    a) to raise the idea of inequality central to Fitzgerald's novel
    b) to celebrate Fitzgerald as a great novelist
    c) to praise Fitzgerald's economic insights
    d) to condemn the inequality of the Roaring Twenties

WRITING AND DISCUSSION

A. How far apart are the haves and the have-nots in the United States?

1. **Discuss**: Look closely at Figure 1.3, "The New Wealth Divide in the United States," in the Saez/Zucman excerpt. In the notes to the figure, Saez and Zucman explain that the "scales differ by a factor of 100 to reflect the fact that [the] top 1 percent of families are 100 times richer than the bottom 90 percent of families." What does this mean exactly? *Use Table 1.1 to think through the way this chart works and make sense of the numbers.*

2. **Discuss**: Based on your analysis of Figure 1.3, would you say that the United States is a place of great economic equality or inequality? How much does your answer to this question depend on the time period under consideration?

3. **Discuss**: What difference does it make, according to Vandivier, if you are born into a poor family versus a wealthy family? According to The Great Gatsby Curve, in which countries is it easiest for a poor child to "climb the economic ladder"? In which countries is it most difficult for a poor child to do the same?

4. **Write**: Many people argue that the United States is the land of opportunity where a poor child can work hard and achieve great success. Would Saez, Zucman, Vandivier, and Krueger agree or disagree? What do the two studies suggest about the likelihood of a child born in poverty moving up the economic ladder? How do you feel about the research you have learned about here? *Use evidence from Saez, Zucman, Vandivier, and Krueger in your response.*

Table 1.1 is available for download at www.usinginformationaltext.com/student.

B. Does wealth make all the difference in Gatsby?

1. **Discuss**: In "What Is The Great Gatsby Curve," David Vandivier quotes Alan Krueger on the "advantages and disadvantages of income passed from parents to the children." What sorts of advantages and disadvantages of income and wealth do we see in Tom and Nick (chapter 1) and Gatsby (chapter 6)? How are these three characters shaped by what their families can and cannot provide for them? *Use Table 1.2 to collect and organize your evidence.*

2. **Write**: Does wealth make all the difference in *Gatsby*? How are the three main male characters, Nick, Gatsby, and Tom, advantaged and disadvantaged by the family circumstances in which they happen to be born? Does *Gatsby* reinforce for you the economic lessons of income inequality and The Great Gatsby Curve as outlined in the readings? Or does it make you feel that life is more complicated than economics? *Use evidence from Vandivier and* Gatsby *in your response.*

Table 1.2 is available for download at www.usinginformationaltext.com/student.

C. Is Gatsby a victim of The Great Gatsby Curve?

1. **Discuss**: Compare the experiences of Tom Buchanan at Yale (chapter 1) with Gatsby at St. Olaf College (chapter 6). How do their different experiences reflect the levels of economic inequality of the period?

2. **Discuss**: Think about what we know about how Gatsby makes money (chapters 6 and 7). Do you see his success as a reflection of his ability or inability to climb the economic ladder? Why? Think in particular about the contrast between Tom's, Nick's, and Gatsby's careers. *Use Table 1.3 to collect and organize your responses.*

3. **Research**: Saez and Zucman write briefly about the relation between wealth inequality and "the inherited fortunes of the robber barons of the Gilded Age." Research the robber barons of the Gilded Age. In what ways did they earn their great wealth? How might Tom's father and grandfather have obtained the money he inherited from them?

4. **Write**: In your opinion, is Gatsby a victim of The Great Gatsby Curve? Does his economic progress confirm or reject the predictions of The Great Gatsby Curve? How does Gatsby's experience with money compare with Tom's (and Nick's)? *Use evidence from* Gatsby *and the readings to make an argument about what Gatsby's economic fortunes reflect about the possibility of moving up the American economic ladder.*

Table 1.3 is available for download at www.usinginformationaltext.com/student.

CLASS ACTIVITY 1

Task: All of *Gatsby* is told from the perspective of Nick. Aside from dialogue, we know very little about how the other characters, particularly the minor characters, think about the characters and events of the story. Use what you have learned about inequality to think about how some of the less-advantaged characters within the novel might view and discuss their more privileged peers and any of the events in the text.

Pick one of the following characters and write a scene in which that character narrates one of the events of the novel:

- The young Greek, Michaelis, who runs the "coffee joint" by the "ashheaps" (chapter 7)
- The policeman who answers the call at the accident (chapter 7)
- Gatsby's father
- The caddy who witnesses Jordan's cheating at golf (chapter 3)
- The man who sells Mrs. Wilson the dog (chapter 2)
- The elevator boy in Tom's (and Mrs. Wilson's) apartment in New York (chapter 2)
- Mr. McKee, the neighbor and photographer (chapter 2)
- The janitor at the apartment in New York (chapter 2) who fetches sandwiches

1. **Write your scene**: Your scene may be a retelling of an existing scene (the policeman retells the scene of his initial investigation of the accident, from his perspective) or a new scene based on events in the novel (Mr. McKee narrates the discussion he has with his wife after the visit with Tom, Nick, and Mrs. Wilson). Try to enrich your scene with specific details from *Gatsby*, but infuse it as well with your sense of how your character would view the actions and behavior of the privileged elite of the novel.

2. **Reflection**: Write a reflection in which you explain what you were trying to accomplish with your new scene. Justify (with textual evidence) your choices. Explain how your scene reflects your understanding of Fitzgerald's text as well as your insights about how your character's views might be shaped by his or her sense of place and potential in the vastly unequal world of *Gatsby*. Use and cite evidence from both the novel and the readings to explain how your character views wealth inequality in the world of *Gatsby*, how he or she assesses the actions of the main (and wealthy) characters, and how he or she sees relations between the rich and everyone else.

May be photocopied for classroom use. *Using Informational Text to Teach* The Great Gatsby by Audrey Fisch and Susan Chenelle © 2018 (Lanham, MD: Rowman & Littlefield).

CLASS ACTIVITY 1 RUBRIC

Category	4—Excellent	3—Good	2—Satisfactory	1—Unsatisfactory
Scene (presentation of knowledge and ideas)	Scene demonstrates strong and insightful comprehension of the novel and the issues in the informational texts	Scene demonstrates solid comprehension of the novel and the issues in the informational texts	Scene demonstrates some comprehension of the novel and the issues in the informational texts, though the scene may be vague or ineffective	Scene does not demonstrate comprehension of the novel and the issues in the informational texts
Reflection (cite relevant and sufficient textual evidence)	Reflection makes clear, insightful arguments based on substantial specific evidence from the novel and informational texts	Reflection makes clear arguments based on specific evidence from the novel and informational texts	Reflection makes arguments that may be vague or not clearly based on evidence from the novel and informational texts	Reflection does not make arguments based on evidence from the novel and informational texts
Vocabulary (use domain-specific vocabulary)	Several "words to own" from the unit are used correctly in your scene and/or reflection	Some "words to own" from the unit are used correctly in your scene and/or reflection	One or more "words to own" from the unit are used in your scene and/or reflection but perhaps not correctly or effectively	No "words to own" from the unit are used in your scene and/or reflection

May be photocopied for classroom use. *Using Informational Text to Teach* The Great Gatsby by Audrey Fisch and Susan Chenelle © 2018 (Lanham, MD: Rowman & Littlefield).

Documentation and style (in-text citation and works cited)	Reflection conforms to the appropriate style guidelines (MLA) for in-text citation and works cited; scene follows appropriate style and format for a section of a novel	Reflection conforms with limited errors to the appropriate style guidelines (MLA) for in-text citation and works cited; scene follows appropriate style and format for a section of a novel with limited errors	Reflection attempts to conform to the appropriate style guidelines (MLA) for in-text citation and works cited but does so ineffectively or inaccurately; scene attempts to follow appropriate style and format for a section of a novel but does so ineffectively or inaccurately	Reflection does not conform to the appropriate style guidelines (MLA) for in-text citation and works cited; scene does not follow appropriate style and format for a section of a novel

CLASS ACTIVITY 2

Task: *Gatsby* is cited by both the readings in this unit and by many other great writers and thinkers as a particularly powerful illustration of the danger of excessive wealth and economic inequality. Imagine F. Scott Fitzgerald, Emmanuel Saez, Gabriel Zucman, David Vandivier, and Alan Krueger are invited to the White House with the newly elected president for a discussion of inequality, public policy, and economic mobility in the United States. What ideas will each of these thinkers present? (You may or may not want to include characters from *Gatsby* in this conversation, depending on the size of the groups.)

1. **Choose your roles and draft your testimony.** Each student will take on a particular role. Use your understanding of the reading and *Gatsby* to draft your remarks and to anticipate the sorts of questions and comments other characters may ask or offer.

2. **Conduct your White House meeting.** You may choose to film your meeting and present that film to the class. Or you may choose to perform the hearing as a live conversation. Be sure that your character uses information from the readings and *Gatsby* in his remarks.

3. **Reflection**: Write a reflection in which you explain what you were trying to convey during the White House meeting with your character's testimony and why. Justify your decisions with textual evidence from the readings and *Gatsby*. Explain how your testimony demonstrates your understanding of the issues of economic inequality as reflected in the readings and *Gatsby*.

4. **Post-White House meeting presidential address**: Write a brief statement by the newly elected president explaining his or her views on the issue of economic inequality. Will the new president cite *Gatsby* and Fitzgerald in his or her remarks about the United States today? How will he or she address the issue of rising economic inequality and diminishing economic mobility? Use what the president has learned from the White House meeting to craft his or her statement.

May be photocopied for classroom use. *Using Informational Text to Teach* The Great Gatsby by Audrey Fisch and Susan Chenelle © 2018 (Lanham, MD: Rowman & Littlefield).

CLASS ACTIVITY 2 RUBRIC

Category	4—Excellent	3—Good	2—Satisfactory	1—Unsatisfactory
Testimony (presentation of knowledge and ideas)	Testimony demonstrates strong and insightful comprehension of the issues at stake through ample, effective use of evidence from the novel and the informational texts	Testimony demonstrates solid comprehension of the issues at stake through frequent, effective use of evidence from the novel and the informational texts	Testimony demonstrates some comprehension of the issues at stake through occasional, though perhaps vague or ineffective, use of evidence from the novel and the informational texts	Testimony does not demonstrate comprehension of the issues at stake through use of evidence from the novel and/or the informational texts
Reflection (cite relevant and sufficient textual evidence)	Reflection makes clear, insightful arguments based on substantial specific evidence from the novel and informational texts	Reflection makes clear arguments based on specific evidence from the novel and informational texts	Reflection makes arguments that may be vague or not clearly based on evidence from the novel and informational texts	Reflection does not make arguments based on evidence from the novel and informational texts
Presidential address (presentation of knowledge and ideas)	Presidential address demonstrates strong and insightful comprehension of the issues at stake through ample, effective use of evidence from the novel, the informational texts, and the White House meeting	Presidential address demonstrates solid comprehension of the issues at stake through frequent, effective use of evidence from the novel, the informational texts, and the White House meeting	Presidential address demonstrates some comprehension of the issues at stake through occasional, though perhaps vague or ineffective, use of evidence from the novel, the informational texts, and the White House meeting	Presidential address does not demonstrate comprehension of the issues at stake through use of evidence from the novel, the informational texts, and the White House meeting

May be photocopied for classroom use. *Using Informational Text to Teach* The Great Gatsby by Audrey Fisch and Susan Chenelle © 2018 (Lanham, MD: Rowman & Littlefield).

Category	4—Excellent	3—Good	2—Satisfactory	1—Unsatisfactory
Vocabulary (use domain-specific vocabulary)	Several "words to own" from the unit are used correctly in the testimony, reflection, and/or presidential address	Some "words to own" from the unit are used correctly in the testimony, reflection, and/or presidential address	One or more "words to own" from the unit are used in the testimony, reflection, and/or presidential address but perhaps not correctly or effectively	No "words to own" from the unit are used in the testimony, reflection, and/or presidential address
Documentation and style (in-text citation and works cited)	Reflection and presidential address conform to the appropriate style guidelines (MLA) for in-text citation and works cited	Reflection and presidential address conform with limited errors to the appropriate style guidelines (MLA) for in-text citation and works cited	Reflection and presidential address attempt to conform to the appropriate style guidelines (MLA) for in-text citation and works cited but do so ineffectively or inaccurately	Reflection and presidential address do not conform to the appropriate style guidelines (MLA) for in-text citation and works cited

May be photocopied for classroom use. *Using Informational Text to Teach* The Great Gatsby by Audrey Fisch and Susan Chenelle © 2018 (Lanham, MD: Rowman & Littlefield).

UNIT 2

What Is Tom Buchanan Worried About—Is Civilization "Going to Pieces"?

TEACHER'S GUIDE
Overview

Gatsby is centered around wealthy white people but also around a clash between a privileged white world and the working-class, ethnic, and racial Others at the margins of that world. The language of racism and anti-Semitism can be difficult for students to unpack without some broader understanding of the larger cultural climate of American nativism in which *Gatsby* sits.

To explore these issues, we have selected two readings, both alluded to by Fitzgerald in *Gatsby*, which highlight the ways in which even people such as Tom, at the apex of power and wealth, feel threatened by others and worried about a decline of white civilization. The excerpts from Lothrop Stoddard, whom Tom calls Goddard, and from Kenneth L. Roberts, writing in the *Saturday Evening Post*, which Tom and Jordan read, allow students to think broadly about Fitzgerald's representation of this white civilization.

Some of the more challenging discussion and writing prompts ask students to think about whether Fitzgerald is reflecting, endorsing, or critiquing the cultural nativism and white supremacy we see in evidence in the text.

TIMING

Chapters 1 and 2 contain the allusions to the two readings under consideration in this unit. Racism and anti-Semitism also emerge significantly in chapters 4, 7, and 9.

Consider the following guidelines regarding when to undertake the different activities:

Essential Question for Discussion and Writing	Objective	Suggested Timing	Suggested Rubric	Additional Research
A. How does Stoddard craft his argument? RI 1, 2, 3, 4, 5, 6, 8, 10 W 1, 2, 4, 5, 9, 10 SL 1, 4 L 1, 2, 3, 5, 6	SW analyze Stoddard's use of language in order to write an essay discussing how he uses figurative language and rhetoric to shape his argument.	Any time—this set of questions doesn't require any knowledge of *Gatsby*.	A	N
B. What danger do "mongrels" pose to the white race? RL 1, 2, 3, 4, 5, 10 RI 1, 2, 3, 4, 5, 6, 9, 10 W 1, 2, 4, 5, 9, 10 SL 1, 4 L 1, 2, 3, 5, 6	SW will use Stoddard and Roberts to analyze fears articulated in *Gatsby* about the mongrelization of the white race.	After chapter 1, when Tom, Daisy, Nick, and Miss Baker discuss the "white race," and chapter 2, or when Myrtle buys the "mongrel" dog and she and Catherine McKee engage in a conversation about marriage and breeding complete with racial epithets	A	N
C. What does Wolfsheim represent? RL 1, 2, 3, 4, 5, 6, 10 RI 1, 2, 3, 4, 5, 6, 9, 10 W 1, 2, 4, 5, 9, 10 SL 1, 4 L 1, 2, 3, 5, 6	SW will use Roberts to analyze the anti-Semitic representation of Meyer Wolfsheim.	After chapter 4, when Nick meets Wolfsheim	A	N

Essential Question for Discussion and Writing	Objective	Suggested Timing	Suggested Rubric	Additional Research
D. Who's white? RL 1, 2, 3, 4, 5, 6, 10 RI 1, 2, 3, 4, 5, 6, 9, 10 W 1, 2, 4, 5, 9, 10 SL 1, 4 L 1, 2, 3, 5, 6	SW will consider the idea that Gatsby is Jewish and use that idea, together with Roberts's discussion of the particular threat of Polish Jews, to analyze how the novel participates in anti-Semitism centered around the danger Jews pose to whites.	After students have completed the novel	A	N
E. What is the significance of the people on the margins in *Gatsby*? RL 1, 2, 3, 4, 5, 6, 10 RI 1, 2, 3, 4, 5, 6, 9, 10 W 1, 2, 4, 5, 9, 10 SL 1, 4 L 1, 2, 3, 5, 6	SW will explore the ways in which the racial, ethnic, and class differences of marginal characters serve as a foil to the wealthy white world at the center of *Gatsby*.	If you want students to have a full choice of characters, this assignment needs to be done after students have completed the novel, but students can use this assignment to focus on any of the marginal or secondary characters when they meet them.	A	N
Class Activity				
Film treatment focused on Stoddard's *The Rising Tide of Color Against White World-Supremacy* RL 1, 2, 3, 4, 5, 7, 9, 10 RI 1, 2, 3, 4, 6, 9, 10 W 1, 2, 3, 4, 5, 9, 10 SL 1, 2, 3, 4, 6 L 1, 2, 3, 5, 6	SW write a treatment for the use of the cover image of Stoddard's *The Rising Tide of Color Against White World-Supremacy* along with any accompanying music or sound effects in a new film version of *Gatsby*.	After students have read chapters 2 and 3 with the allusions to Stoddard or after they have completed the novel	Rubric included	N

NOTES ON THE READINGS

- Racism and anti-Semitism are, of course, contentious topics, and teachers may find them challenging to address in the classroom. This unit has been constructed to offer students an opportunity to use the excerpts to think critically about the language and ideas in the text and to see them in their cultural context. Discussing the epithets and racist ideas within the text is certainly better than ignoring them.
- The first excerpt uses extensive figurative language to engage with the idea of the threat to the white world. As a result, it offers students an interesting opportunity to think critically about sophisticated rhetoric employed in the service of racist ideology.
- Anti-Semitism is also a central issue in unit 4: Who Is to Blame in the Black Sox Scandal and in *Gatsby*? Teachers are encouraged to connect the Stoddard and Roberts texts in this unit with the anti-Semitic rhetoric of blame surrounding the role of Jews in the Black Sox scandal.

SUGGESTED MEDIA LINKS

- A variety of cover images for Stoddard's *The Rising Tide of Color Against White World-Supremacy* are available through a Google Images search. Comparative analysis of these can be used as an intriguing opening activity, but we also suggest using these images for our culminating class activity.
- *The Century*, a documentary on America in the twentieth century hosted by Peter Jennings, particularly the end of the second segment and beginning of the third segment on the 1920s, discusses the rise of anti-immigrant sentiment and the Ku Klux Klan (KKK) as an expression of the anxiety felt among white society over the rapid changes brought by modern life. A three-minute segment by Reading Through History also offers an overview of nativism in the 1920s with a great variety of photos and illustrations, focusing on hostility toward Jews, Germans, and southern Italians, and the subsequent legal restrictions on immigration, while a two-minute video from the PTCHistory channel on YouTube focuses more specifically on the KKK and laws that restricted immigration. A two-minute segment by United Streaming focuses on the violence of the KKK and the racist sentiments behind the enacted immigration quotas.

- A November 2015 *Democracy Now* segment examines the parallels between the present-day controversy over accepting Syrian refugees and opposition in the 1930s to accepting Jewish refugees fleeing the Nazis. The video features polls from the late 1930s showing that a majority of Americans opposed proposals to accept thousands of German, largely Jewish, refugee children, noting that Anne Frank was among those children denied entry to the United States.
- Maria Hinojosa's *America by the Numbers* is a fascinating eight-part PBS documentary series, exploring demographic changes in the United States. Sharing just the sixty-second trailer about demographic changes in Clarkson, Georgia, will allow students to see how tensions about the future of the white world from the 1920s persist today. Supplemental educational materials for the series, including questions centered around reading and using statistics, are also available through the Teaching Tolerance project of the Southern Poverty Law Center.
- A May 2016 National Public Radio interview with former presidential candidate Pat Buchanan echoes Stoddard's concerns that whites will cease to be the majority race in America by the mid-twenty-first century. Teachers wishing to avoid speaking directly about President Donald Trump can focus on Buchanan's ideas from the middle of the six-minute interview, which are particularly relevant to Stoddard's and Roberts's sense of the danger immigration poses to the white world. Students can analyze the resonance with Stoddard and Roberts of Buchanan's praise of a "time-out," after 1920, during which "all those folks from Eastern and Southern Europe were assimilated and Americanized."
- The 2016 presidential campaign provided often startling resonance with the ideas expressed in these excerpts. Video and audio clips of candidate and President Donald Trump's views on immigration are readily available online.

VOCABULARY WARM-UP

WORDS TO OWN: assimilation, dissipated, elements, hegemony, hybrid, influx, integrated, mongrel, myriad, oblivion, parasites, rent, supremacy, unscathed

Section A: Use context clues: Read the following sentences and use context clues to determine the meaning of the italicized words.

1. I hope to emerge from high school *unscathed*, but that may be difficult given how difficult adolescence is and how damaging this period in life can be for many young people. Can you think of any of your peers whom you fear will not emerge from high school *unscathed*? What strategies do you employ to remain *unscathed*?

2. Different metaphors of *assimilation* in the United States exist. If we think about the United States as a melting pot, the idea is that each immigrant group contributes its unique difference and flavor to create a generally uniform whole in which the group is *assimilated* into the whole. Some prefer the idea of the United States as a salad bowl, in which each group contributes to the American salad over all, but the unique flavor and difference of each ingredient remains despite the process of *assimilation*. Which metaphor of *assimilation* appeals to you and why?

3. Those who value genetic purity above all else might reject a dog as a *mongrel* or a mutt. Labradors and poodles are purebreds, whereas labradoodles might be *mongrels* to some but the best of both breeds to others. What do you think is behind labels such as *mongrel* or mutt?

4. My friend might claim that I am a *parasite* because I always ask her for rides to school. But maybe it is she who benefits because I keep her company, and my companionship makes her a safer driver. Would you call me a *parasite*? Why or why not?

5. Some people think the world would be a better place if the United States exerted its influence over other nations. Others think that American *hegemony* is arrogant and misguided and that the United States should worry about its own problems. What do you think about American *hegemony*? Do you think the United States' size and power bring a responsibility for global leadership?

6. A *hybrid* car uses a mix of electricity and gasoline for power, and many people like them because they require less gas and are less harmful to the environment. For Roberts, a "*hybrid* race of peoples" would be "worthless." What do you think Roberts means by a "*hybrid* race of peoples"? Why do you think he might see such a "race" as "worthless"?

Section B: More context clues: Here your task is to use context clues to understand the italicized word's meaning AND to practice your context clues skills.

1. Stoddard writes, "Even if laws are passed tomorrow so drastic as to shut out permanently the *influx* of undesirable elements, it will yet take several generations before the combined action of assimilation and elimination shall have restabilized our population." By *influx*, Stoddard means

   a) inflow
   b) outflow
   c) unhealthy
   d) illegal

2. Which word(s) from the sentence in Question 1 best help(s) the reader understand the meaning of *influx*?

   a) shut out
   b) laws
   c) undesirable
   d) several generations

3. Roberts writes, "If more and more immigrants continue to pour in, and assimilation continues badly, one of two things will inevitably happen: either the United States will develop large numbers of separate racial groups . . . or America will be populated by a *mongrel* race entirely different from the present American people as we know them to-day." By *mongrel*, Roberts means

   a) ugly
   b) racist
   c) racially mixed
   d) immigrant

4. Which word(s) from the sentence in Question 3 best help(s) you understand the meaning of *mongrel*?

   a) more and more
   b) separate racial groups
   c) two things
   d) badly

5. Roberts writes, "The American nation was founded and developed by the Nordic race, but if a few more million members of the Alpine, Mediterranean and Semitic races are poured among us, the result must inevitably be a *hybrid* race of people . . . worthless . . . mongrels." By his use of the word *hybrid*, Roberts is suggesting the resulting *hybrid* race of people will be

   a) powerful
   b) impure and inferior
   c) superior and valuable
   d) pure

6. Which word(s) from the sentence in Question 5 best help(s) you understand how Roberts is using the term *hybrid*?

   a) American nation was founded and developed
   b) worthless . . . mongrels
   c) the result
   d) members of the Alpine, Mediterranean, and Semitic races

---

May be photocopied for classroom use. *Using Informational Text to Teach* The Great Gatsby by Audrey Fisch and Susan Chenelle © 2018 (Lanham, MD: Rowman & Littlefield).

Section C: Sometimes common words are used in uncommon ways. **Use the dictionary** in order to understand the uncommon meanings of the italicized common words.

1. A chemist might talk about the different *elements* that make up a particular compound, such as water being made of hydrogen and oxygen. If one thinks of society as being made up of different *elements*, what would those *elements* be? Does it make sense to you to think about society as made up of different *elements*? Why or why not?

2. If you *rent* your home, you pay a monthly *rent* to your landlord. If your shirt is *rent*, it may cost you money, but not because you have to pay a landlord. What does it mean for a piece of clothing to be *rent*?

Section D: Use the dictionary to look up the italicized words and answer the following questions based on their definitions.

1. Stoddard argues that "the planet was *integrated* under the *hegemony* of a single race with a common civilization." How is Stoddard using the term *integrated*? Do you think all races functioned cooperatively and on equal footing under the *hegemony* of a single race? Can you imagine which single race exerted its *hegemony* over the others?

2. In South Africa, ideas about white *supremacy* supported the apartheid system, in which white people enjoyed far greater rights and privileges than black or mixed-race people. Why do you think white *supremacy* has been such a powerful ideology?

3. As more and more colleges become test-optional, could the SAT be in danger of *oblivion*? How do you think the College Board might defend the SAT from fading into *oblivion*?

4. College applications ask for *myriad* examples of achievement. Do you find this requirement an unnecessary burden or a welcome opportunity to demonstrate your *myriad* accomplishments? Explain.

5. People often feel very enthusiastic when making a New Year's resolution or starting a new exercise program, but their determination tends to *dissipate* fairly quickly. Why do you think some people can't keep their passion for their goals from *dissipating*?

6. The Borg on *Star Trek* are known for their particular version of *assimilation*. Their mantra sums it up: "We are the Borg. Lower your shields and surrender your ships. We will add your biological and technological distinctiveness to our own. Your culture will adapt to service us. Resistance is futile." As the Borg *assimilate* different species, what happens to that species' culture and distinctiveness? Do you think the makers of *Star Trek* were offering the Borg as a critique of certain kinds of *assimilation*? Explain.

7. In some cultures, it is customary for mourners to wear *rent* clothing during a period of mourning. What do you think of this custom? What do you think the wearing of *rent* clothing might symbolize?

Section E: Practice using the word correctly by choosing the correct form of the word that best fits in the blank within the following sentences.

1. I was hoping the clouds would ____ and the day would turn bright and sunny.

   a) dissipated
   b) dissipate
   c) dissipating
   d) dissipates

2. As we welcome immigrants to our country, we need to think carefully about the process of ___; immigrants need to be able to retain their customs and traditions even as they learn about and take on new American ways.

   a) assimilates
   b) assimilation
   c) assimilate
   d) assimilated

3. Some people think campaign finance reform is critical to our democracy; currently, super PACs and big donors are able to exert their ____ through big money in politics.

   a) hegemonic
   b) hegemon
   c) hegemony
   d) hegemonies

4. The two had a ____ relationship; he thrived off of her attention and care, but she didn't receive anything in return.

   a) parasite
   b) parasites
   c) parasitic
   d) parasitically

5 Some say our neighborhood has been ____; I would argue that the influx of immigrants from all around the world has brought much needed new energy and culture to our previously boring area of the city.

   a) mongrelized
   b) mongrel
   c) mongrels
   d) mongrelization

6. Do you think the music of Prince will be with us forever or will his work fall into ____ in the generations to come?

   a) oblivious
   b) oblivion
   c) oblivions
   d) obliviate

Section F: Vocabulary skits

Use the model sentences and definitions to understand the words in question. Create a skit in which you address the given topic. Every member of the group must use the vocabulary word at least once during your performance of the skit.

1. *myriad*—many persons or things

    - The *myriad* examples of bullying that students suffer every day require us to take action.
    - Despite my *myriad* experiences with young adults, I was completely unprepared to handle this particular crisis.
    - My homework can feel endless; there are seemingly *myriad* assignments to do, pages to read, and essays to write.

Scenario: Create a skit in which the student council takes on the issue of bullying. Members can discuss the *myriad* ways to address bullying, and they may or may not feel that bullying can be reduced.

2. *hegemony*—leadership, influence over others

    - Do you think it is possible for students to take a more active role in school leadership and challenge the *hegemony* of school administrators?
    - Google has had a *hegemonic* place in the technology world, but will its dominance continue?
    - It can be difficult to make change in the world, but if each of us stands up to the forces that be, perhaps we can challenge the status quo and the current *hegemony* of the rich and powerful.

Scenario: Create a skit in which a group of actors debate the *hegemony* of Hollywood studios. Is it possible to create content as an independent artist and achieve success? Can one make it as an artist outside of and perhaps challenging the *hegemony* of Hollywood? Or are the forces of Hollywood *hegemony* too powerful?

May be photocopied for classroom use. *Using Informational Text to Teach* The Great Gatsby by Audrey Fisch and Susan Chenelle © 2018 (Lanham, MD: Rowman & Littlefield).

3. *mongrel*—an animal of mixed breed; more broadly, a combination formed out of different entities

- One might call the United States a *mongrel* nation; we are formed out of the cultures and skills of people from all over the world.
- Because my parents are different races, the girl called me a *mongrel*; I called her a racist.
- Some people are highly sensitive to the infusion of new words into the English language; however, we might celebrate the *mongrelization* of our language as a sign of the rich diversity of peoples who now speak English.

Scenario: When Mildred and Richard Loving, an African American woman and a white man, married in 1958, they violated Virginia law. Their case went to the Supreme Court, where the court overturned Virginia law and affirmed their right to marry. The couple had three children: Donald, Peggy, and Sidney. Imagine these three now-adult descendants of Mildred and Richard come to your school to discuss the ways in which they were tormented as *mongrels* growing up in a world in which mixed-race children were disparaged. How will they describe their experience? What questions will the students in the audience ask?

ESSENTIAL QUESTION: WHAT IS TOM BUCHANAN WORRIED ABOUT— IS CIVILIZATION "GOING TO PIECES"?

Introduction to the Unit

This is a challenging unit dealing with some difficult and uncomfortable ideas that were commonplace during the time of *Gatsby*. First, we read an excerpt from Lothrop Stoddard, a well-known advocate of white *supremacy*. His views of the threat of immigrants and nonwhites to white *supremacy* are referenced by Tom Buchanan; Gatsby also possesses volume 1 of Stoddard's lectures, albeit with uncut pages, in his library.

The second reading echoes Stoddard in worrying about the danger to white society of immigration and assimilation. Kenneth L. Roberts's focus on Jewish immigrants as criminals is particularly helpful in thinking about the character of Meyer Wolfsheim. Together, the two readings in this section begin to unearth the racist and anti-Semitic underside of the glamorous world of *Gatsby*.

READING #1: EXCERPT FROM *THE RISING TIDE OF COLOR AGAINST WHITE WORLD-SUPREMACY*

Introduction

According to scholar Ronald Berman, Lothrop Stoddard was a household name in the United States, and his ideas were widely publicized in the news media of the time and even cited by President Harding. Stoddard articulates his view that white civilization, both in Europe and the United States, is endangered by the advancement of what he calls "the colored world." That Fitzgerald cited Stoddard (as

---

Reflect on the essential question: What does the question suggest to you?

Research and reflect on the introduction: What do you know about the history of white supremacy in the United States? When did white supremacy thrive? Hint: look at the history of the KKK. Why do you think white supremacist and anti-immigrant ideas might have been popular in the 1920s? In what ways do you think this sort of thinking persists today?

Reflect on the title: "The Rising Tide of Color Against White World-Supremacy." Based on the title, what do you think is the subject of this piece of writing? What can you perceive about the perspective of the author? What does the image of a rising tide suggest about how the author feels about the "Rising Tide of Color"? Whose world supremacy is the tide of color rising against?

Reflect on the introduction: If Stoddard was a household name, whose ideas were part of mainstream discourse and even cited by a U.S. president, what do you think that means? Do you think everyone in the United States shared Goddard's views?

May be photocopied for classroom use. *Using Informational Text to Teach* The Great Gatsby by Audrey Fisch and Susan Chenelle © 2018 (Lanham, MD: Rowman & Littlefield).

Goddard) and his book (as *The Rise of the Coloured Empires*) makes clear that Stoddard and his racist, white supremacist ideas were part of mainstream discourse in the Twenties.

From *The Rising Tide of Color Against White World-Supremacy* by Lothrop Stoddard

[Stoddard identifies World War I, which ended in 1918, and its effect on white Europeans, as central to the challenges facing Europe.]

Such is Europe's deplorable condition as she staggers forth from the hideous ordeal of the Great War; her . . . capital *dissipated*, . . . her industrial fabric *rent* and tattered, her finances threatened with bankruptcy, the flower of her manhood dead on the battle-field, her populations devitalized and discouraged, her children stunted by malnutrition. A sombre picture.

And Europe is the white homeland, the heart of the white world. The colored world remains virtually *unscathed*.

Here is the truth of the matter: The white world to-day stands at the crossroads of life and death. A fever has racked the white frame and undermined its constitution.

Our world is too vigorous for even the Great War, of itself, to prove a mortal wound.

The white world thus still has its choice. But it must be a positive choice. Decisions—firm decisions—must be made. Constructive measures—drastic measures—must be taken. Above all: time presses, and drift is fatal. The tide ebbs. The swimmer must put forth strong strokes to reach the shore. Else—swift *oblivion* in the dark ocean.

Reflect: In the opening selection, Stoddard uses colorful language to paint what he calls a "sombre picture" of the state of Europe after World War I. What are the key images in this picture? Think through each of the images here. For example, why is Europe staggering? What does it mean for Europe's capital to be dissipated? What is an industrial fabric and how can it be rent and tattered? What do you think it means for a population to be devitalized? What is Stoddard's point about the current conditions in Europe?

Key idea: Stoddard contrasts post-world war Europe, which he calls the "white homeland," with the "colored world." What point is he making with this contrast?

Notice Stoddard's language use. He imagines the white world as a person with a fever and as a swimmer in the ocean. How do Stoddard's language choices frame his view of the conflict between the white world and the colored world? What do you think the dark ocean represents for Stoddard and why does the swimmer risk oblivion in the dark ocean? What do you think is the effect of this image of the dark ocean?

May be photocopied for classroom use. *Using Informational Text to Teach* The Great Gatsby by Audrey Fisch and Susan Chenelle © 2018 (Lanham, MD: Rowman & Littlefield).

[Moving his attention from Europe to the United States, Stoddard identifies immigration as central to what he sees as a racial crisis in the United States.]

Even if laws are passed tomorrow so drastic as to shut out permanently the *influx* of undesirable *elements*, it will yet take several generations before the combined action of *assimilation* and elimination shall have restabilized our population. . . .

We are in for generations of racial readjustment. . . . We will probably never . . . be the race we might have been if America had been reserved for the descendants of the picked Nordics of colonial times.

But that is no reason for folding our hands in despairing inaction. On the contrary, we should be up and doing, for though some of our race-heritage has been lost, more yet remains. We can still be a very great people—if we will it so. . . .

One fact should be clearly understood: If America is not true to her own race-soul, she will inevitably lose it. . . .

Vocabulary: Stoddard warns that "drift is fatal." What is drift in the ocean and why is it fatal? How does Stoddard's use of ocean imagery here further his argument about what needs to be done?

Vocabulary: Why do you think Stoddard sees immigrants as an "influx of undesirable elements"? Put this phrase into your own words.

Key idea: Stoddard declares that assimilation and elimination can restabilize the United States. What does he mean? What is the difference between assimilation and elimination?

Key idea: What might America have been, in Stoddard's view, if the country had been reserved for "the descendants of the picked Nordics of colonial times"? Whom do you think he means by his reference to "picked Nordics"?

Key idea: What does Stoddard mean by race-soul? How does his idea link race, soul, and national identity?

If we cheat our country and the world of the splendid promise of American life, we shall have no one to blame but ourselves, and we shall deserve, not pity, but contempt.

[Having laid out what he sees as some of the specific dangers, Stoddard offers broader, more ominous warnings about how white civilization is in danger.]

Ours is a solemn moment. We stand at a crisis—the *supreme* crisis of the ages. For unnumbered millenniums man has toiled upward from the dank jungles of savagery toward glorious heights which his mental and spiritual potentialities give promise that he shall attain. His path has been slow and wavering. Time and again he has lost his way and plunged into deep valleys. Man's trail is littered with the wrecks of dead civilizations and dotted with the graves of promising peoples stricken by an untimely end.

Humanity has thus suffered many a disaster. . . . Out of the prehistoric shadows the white races pressed to the front and proved in *myriad* ways their fitness for the *hegemony* of mankind. Gradually they forged a common civilization; then, . . . they spread over the earth, filling its empty spaces with their superior breeds. . . .

Three centuries later the whites took a fresh leap forward. The nineteenth century was a new age of discovery—this time into the realms of science. The hidden powers of nature were unveiled, incalculable energies were tamed to human use and at last the planet was *integrated* under the *hegemony* of a single race with a common civilization.

> **Key idea:** How does Stoddard imagine human progress? Where does Stoddard place the origins of humanity? How does he describe the process of civilization? Why is humanity currently at a crisis?
>
> **Vocabulary:** What does Stoddard mean by the "hegemony of mankind"? Put this into your own words. Why does he think the white races have proved their fitness for the hegemony of mankind?
>
> **Notice** that Stoddard uses the plural to describe both the "white races" and the "superior breeds" spreading over the earth. Why? Who are these breeds? We think about breeds of dogs and breeds of horses; what does Stoddard's language suggest about how he thinks about differences among humans?

May be photocopied for classroom use. *Using Informational Text to Teach* The Great Gatsby by Audrey Fisch and Susan Chenelle © 2018 (Lanham, MD: Rowman & Littlefield).

. . . All these marvellous achievements were due solely to superior heredity, and the mere maintenance of what had been won depended absolutely upon the prior maintenance of race-values. . . .

If the present drift be not changed, we whites are all ultimately doomed. Unless we set our house in order, the doom will sooner or later overtake us all.

And that would mean that the race obviously endowed with the greatest creative ability, the race which had achieved most in the past and which gave the richer promise for the future, had passed away, carrying with it to the grave those potencies upon which the realization of man's highest hopes depends. A million years of human evolution might go uncrowned, and earth's *supreme* life-product, man, might never fulfil his potential destiny. This is why we today face "The Crisis of the Ages."

Stoddard, Lothrop. *The Rising Tide of Color Against White World-Supremacy.* Blue Ribbon Books, 1920.

Key idea: Stoddard suggests that the world became integrated under the hegemony of a single race in the nineteenth century. How is he using the term "integrated" here? What does he mean by a common civilization and how does this idea relate to his sense of the crisis facing Europe and America?

Key idea: For Stoddard, what was responsible for the marvelous achievements of the nineteenth century?

Key idea: Why, according to Stoddard, might whites be doomed?

Key idea: Why, for Stoddard, does this moment represent the crisis of the ages?

Notice how Stoddard uses the term "man" in this final paragraph. How is he using this term? Whose destiny is he worried about?

Reflect: What seems to be Stoddard's purpose in writing this book? How do you think he would have wanted his readers to respond? Why do you think his views might have been acceptable in the 1920s?

READING #2: EXCERPT FROM MATERIAL THAT FIRST APPEARED AS ARTICLES IN THE *SATURDAY EVENING POST* AND THEN AS A BOOK, *WHY EUROPE LEAVES HOME*

Introduction

Whereas Stoddard focuses on the danger of immigration and the "colored races" generally, the excerpt from Kenneth L. Roberts, whose ideas were published in the mainstream and well-read *Saturday Evening Post*, reflect the particular ways in which Jewish immigrants were stereotyped and viewed as a threat. In *Gatsby*, Jordan reads to Tom from this periodical. The end of the excerpt below makes clear that Jews are not considered part of the "Nordic" or white race and echoes Stoddard's rhetoric about the danger to white civilization in similarly ugly terms.

**From *Why Europe Leaves Home*
by Kenneth L. Roberts**

Even the most liberal-minded authorities on immigration state that the Jews of Poland are human *parasites*, living on one another and on their neighbors of other races by means which too often are underhanded, that they continue to exist in the same way after coming to America, and that they are therefore highly undesirable as immigrants. Even now, in Central Europe, when a thing is accomplished in a dishonest or illegal manner, it is spoken of as being done *Jüdischer Weise*, or in the Jewish manner. This is pointed out by Captain P. Wright in the report of the British Mission to Poland—a British government publication. . . .

Reflect on the introduction: The introduction suggests that Jewish immigrants were considered a threat to white civilization. How does the introduction change the way you think about whiteness? Which other ethnic groups, do you think, were once considered outside the white race? Are you surprised to learn that the idea of whiteness has changed over time?

Reflect on the title: *Why Europe Leaves Home*. Based on the title, what can you infer about the subject of this piece? In writing for a general audience in the *Saturday Evening Post*, what do you think Roberts's purpose was?

Reflect on the opening sentence and paragraph: The excerpt begins very directly with a full-on attack about the nature of Jews in Poland. What stereotype does Roberts offer about Polish Jews?

Notice that Roberts cites "liberal-minded authorities" and Captain P. Wright. Why do you think he does this? What does it mean to be "liberal-minded"? How do these citations serve to back Roberts's claims?

Luftgeschaft means "air business." Among the German, Polish and Russian Jews there are literally thousands who have no business at all, and no regular income. They turn a penny honestly or dishonestly whenever or wherever they can; and even the Jews themselves will admit that they do it dishonestly far more often than they do it honestly. This is "air business." It is a calling which is peculiar to Jews in Central Europe; and the people who follow it are called *Luftmenschen* or "air men." They are the true human *parasites*; and great numbers of them are found among the emigrants from Poland to America. Landing in America when jobs are hard to get they will at once start their air business—just as so many thousands of them have done in the past. . . .

Assimilation hadn't been any too good in the United States for the twenty years prior to the war. If more and more immigrants continue to pour in, and *assimilation* continues badly, one of two things will inevitably happen: either the United States will develop large numbers of separate racial groups . . . or America will be populated by a *mongrel* race entirely different from the present American people as we know them to-day. . . .

> **Key idea:** Roberts describes Central European Jews as "human parasites." Why? Why do you think some Jews might have engaged in what he calls "air business"?
>
> **Key idea:** Roberts describes what he sees as an unsuccessful history of assimilation of immigrants into the United States. What are the two different outcomes of this unsuccessful assimilation, in his view? In your view, what would be the outcome of successful assimilation, for Roberts?
>
> **Vocabulary:** Why does Roberts use the term "mongrel race" to describe one possibility for the American populace? How is he using the term "mongrel"?

Races cannot be cross-bred without *mongrelization*, any more than breeds of dogs can be cross-bred without *mongrelization*. The American nation was founded and developed by the Nordic race, but if a few more million members of the Alpine, Mediterranean and Semitic races are poured among us, the result must inevitably be a *hybrid* race of people . . . worthless . . . *mongrels*.

Roberts, Kenneth L. *Why Europe Leaves Home*. Bobbs-Merrill Company, 1922.

Vocabulary: Of course dogs *can* be cross-bred successfully, and cross-breeding is often used to create breeds with more favorable characteristics. Labradoodles, for example, are labradors crossed with poodles in order to create a dog that doesn't shed. Roberts, however, uses the term "mongrelization" to condemn cross-breeding of both dogs and people. What do you think of his comparison of humans with dogs here? Why does he see a "hybrid race" as worthless?

Research the terms "Alpine, Mediterranean and Semitic races." (Hint: try Wikipedia.) Where did these ideas about races and racial differences come from? Are you surprised to learn about the different racial classifications for people we would now consider white?

CHECK FOR UNDERSTANDING

1. Stoddard writes, "Here is the truth of the matter: The white world to-day stands at the crossroads of life and death. A fever has racked the white frame and undermined its constitution." Stoddard uses the word *constitution* here to suggest that

    a) American law is under threat.
    b) The white world is lawful.
    c) The white world is in an unhealthy state.
    d) The American constitution needs to be rewritten to address immigration.

2. Which word(s) from the text best help(s) the reader understand Stoddard's use of the term *constitution* in the passage quoted above?

    a) "Here is the truth of the matter"
    b) "The white world today"
    c) "at the crossroads"
    d) "A fever has racked the white frame"

3. Which of the following is NOT one of the points Stoddard makes in the excerpt?

    a) The Great War damaged white Europe.
    b) Immigration is the foundation of the United States.
    c) White civilization controls the planet.
    d) Human achievement by whites is the result of genetic superiority.

4. Stoddards's main goal in *The Rising Tide of Color Against White World-Supremacy* is to

    a) explain the threat to white civilization.
    b) celebrate the achievements of white civilization.
    c) explore the damage done by the Great War.
    d) contrast American and European civilization.

May be photocopied for classroom use. *Using Informational Text to Teach* The Great Gatsby by Audrey Fisch and Susan Chenelle © 2018 (Lanham, MD: Rowman & Littlefield).

5. Which TWO sentences from the text best support the answer to the question above?

   a) "earth's supreme life-product, man, might never fulfil his potential destiny."
   b) "The hidden powers of nature were unveiled, incalculable energies were tamed to human use and at last the planet was integrated under the hegemony of a single race with a common civilization."
   c) "And Europe is the white homeland, the heart of the white world."
   d) "Our world is too vigorous for even the Great War, of itself, to prove a mortal wound."
   e) "All these marvellous achievements were due solely to superior heredity."
   f) "If the present drift be not changed, we whites are all ultimately doomed."

6. Which paraphrase best explains the following quotation from Stoddard: "The hidden powers of nature were unveiled, incalculable energies were tamed to human use and at last the planet was integrated under the hegemony of a single race with a common civilization"?

   a) Whites were able to conquer nature and promote civilization under their rule.
   b) Nature rose up in rebellion against man.
   c) Nature's power is tremendous and cannot be tamed by humans.
   d) Whites intend to create a common civilization.

7. Roberts's purpose in citing Captain P. Wright and the report of the British Mission to Poland is

   a) to add credibility to his ideas.
   b) to contrast his ideas about Jews with those of Captain P. Wright.
   c) to stress the British interest in the issue of Central European Jews.
   d) to compare British views of Jews and Poles.

8. Roberts argues, "Races cannot be cross-bred without mongrelization, any more than breeds of dogs can be cross-bred without mongrelization." Roberts's point of view here suggests that he might support which of the following statements not made in the excerpt?

   a) Blacks and whites should not marry.
   b) Jewish immigration in the United States should be curtailed.
   c) Jewish religious practices should be prohibited.
   d) Jews should be encouraged to enter different professions.

May be photocopied for classroom use. *Using Informational Text to Teach* The Great Gatsby by Audrey Fisch and Susan Chenelle © 2018 (Lanham, MD: Rowman & Littlefield).

9. What is Roberts's goal in discussing the practice he describes as "air business"?

   a) To highlight Jewish contributions in Europe.
   b) To emphasize Jewish criminality.
   c) To stress Jewish success in business.
   d) To underline why assimilation hasn't been successful in the United States.

10. Which TWO examples from the text best illustrate Roberts's goal in relation to the question above?

    a) "Even now, in Central Europe, when a thing is accomplished in a dishonest or illegal manner, it is spoken of as being done *Jüdischer Weise*, or in the Jewish manner."
    b) "great numbers of them are found among the emigrants from Poland to America"
    c) "Assimilation hadn't been any too good in the United States for the twenty years prior to the war."
    d) "They turn a penny honestly or dishonestly whenever or wherever they can"
    e) "Races cannot be cross-bred without mongrelization, any more than breeds of dogs can be cross-bred without mongrelization."

May be photocopied for classroom use. *Using Informational Text to Teach* The Great Gatsby by Audrey Fisch and Susan Chenelle © 2018 (Lanham, MD: Rowman & Littlefield).

WRITING AND DISCUSSION

A. How does Stoddard craft his argument?

Stoddard uses striking figurative language (including distinctive metaphors and images) to grab his reader's attention and assert the seriousness of his concerns about the dangers to white world supremacy.

1. **Discuss**: First, discuss the language Stoddard uses to describe post–World War I conditions in Europe. How does this language contribute to his overall argument? *Use Table 2.1 to record your analysis of Stoddard's language.*

2. **Discuss**: Next, discuss the water imagery Stoddard uses to describe the threat of immigration. How does this language contribute to his overall argument? *Use Table 2.2 to discuss Stoddard's use of language.*

3. **Discuss**: Next, discuss the breeding imagery Stoddard uses to describe the threat to the white race. How does this language contribute to his overall argument? *Use Table 2.3 to discuss Stoddard's use of language.*

4. **Write**: Like all powerful writers, Stoddard uses language carefully to influence his readers. Write a short essay in which you describe and analyze how Stoddard's rhetoric serves to frame his ideas. Consider, then, how powerful language can serve ugly ideas. *Use evidence from Stoddard in your response.*

Tables are available for download at www.usinginformationaltext.com/student.

B. What danger do "mongrels" pose to the white race?

1. **Discuss**: In chapter 1, Tom, Daisy, Nick, and Miss Baker discuss "the white race," Goddard, and the *Saturday Evening Post*. What ideas about race are discussed in this chapter? In what ways do the characters' comments reflect the ideas of the texts by Stoddard and Roberts you have read? *Use Table 2.4 to collect and organize your responses.*

2. **Research**: What breed of dog typically is used or referred to as a "police dog"? Find pictures online of that breed of dog. Compare those pictures with pictures of an Airedale. Does either breed have "startlingly white feet"? What do the pictures of the different breeds of dogs suggest about Tom's and Myrtle's abilities to distinguish a purebred (police dog or Airedale) from a mixed-breed dog?

3. **Discuss**: In chapter 2, Tom buys for Myrtle a dog of "indeterminate breed." Given what you have read in Stoddard and Roberts about the power of the term "mongrel" in ideas about race, consider the significance of this incident. What might the dog symbolize? How might the different characters' attitudes toward the dog reflect their views about race? *Use Table 2.5 to collect and organize your responses.*

4. **Discuss**: In chapter 2, Myrtle and Catherine McKee engage in a conversation about breeding and marriage that features the use of two racist epithets, "gypped" and "kike." How do these words help to define Myrtle and Catherine as characters? How do these particularly ugly words help to define what's at stake in the discussion of marriage in this section?

5. **Write**: What danger do mongrels pose to the white characters of *Gatsby*? Consider the political conversation about the white races in chapter 1 as well as the conversation about marriage in chapter 2. What are Tom and Myrtle worried about? How is the fear of mongrelization represented in the conversation, language, and symbols (such as Myrtle's dog) within *Gatsby*? Use the informational texts in order to place this fear of mongrelization in *Gatsby* within the larger cultural context. *Use evidence from* Gatsby *and the informational texts in your response.*

Tables are available for download at http://www.usinginformationaltext.com/student.

C. What does Wolfsheim represent?

1. **Discuss**: In chapter 4, Nick meets the Jewish gangster Meyer Wolfsheim. Discuss the language Nick uses to describe Wolfsheim and his activities. *Use Table 2.6 to record your analysis of Nick's language.*

2. **Discuss**: Next, compare Nick's description of Wolfsheim and his activities to Roberts's discussion of Jewish immigrants and their air businesses. What similarities do you notice? *Use Table 2.7 to use Roberts's language to analyze the representation of Wolfsheim.*

3. **Discuss**: *Gatsby* is narrated by Nick, whom many critics consider to be an unreliable narrator. Nick's opinions, moreover, cannot be assumed to be shared by Fitzgerald; Nick is Fitzgerald's character but not necessarily his mouthpiece. What do you think Fitzgerald's purpose is in having Nick use the language of anti-Semitism common to the period? Do you think Nick's description of and Fitzgerald's inclusion of Wolfsheim reflect Fitzgerald's anti-Semitism? Or could Fitzgerald be trying to represent and critique the anti-Semitism prevalent in the wealthy society in which Nick travels? Discuss.

4. **Write**: Write a short essay in which you describe and analyze how Nick's description of Wolfsheim takes up and uses anti-Semitic and stereotypical ideas about Jews circulated in the popular media by writers like Roberts. In your opinion, is Fitzgerald reflecting, endorsing, or critiquing the anti-Semitism of Roberts and the culture through his representation of Wolfsheim? Explain. *Use evidence from* Gatsby *and Roberts in your response.*

Tables are available for download at http://www.usinginformationaltext.com/student.

D. Who's white?

1. **Discuss**: In chapter 9, we learn that, among other things, Gatsby changed his name from James (Jimmy) Gatz to Jay Gatsby. Some critics have argued that Gatz is a Jewish name and that Fitzgerald intends Gatsby's name change to be an attempt on Gatsby's part to conceal his Jewish roots. Although the question of whether or not Gatsby is intended to be Jewish has no definitive answer, what does this argument add to your understanding of *Gatsby*?

2. **Discuss**: In the climactic chapter 7, as tensions rise between Tom and Gatsby, Tom again references the threats to white civilization, particularly "intermarriage between black and white." Jordan responds, "We're all white here." If Gatsby is of Jewish descent, would Tom and Jordan consider him white? Why or why not? *Use Roberts's discussion of Jews as you consider this question.*

3. **Discuss**: In the final pages of *Gatsby*, Nick writes, "On the white steps [of Gatsby's house] an obscene word, scrawled by some boy with a piece of brick, stood out clearly in the moonlight and I erased it." Within the context of the anti-Semitism (see the representation of Wolfsheim in chapter 4) and of the obscene words used (see chapter 2) in *Gatsby*, what do you think this obscene word might be? Why do you think Nick doesn't tell us what the word is? Why does he erase it?

4. **Write**: Are all of the main characters in *Gatsby* white? What if they are not? Use your understanding of Roberts and his arguments about the perceived dangers Jews pose to American society to rethink the novel. In what ways is Gatsby a representation of one of those dangerous Jews? How does he threaten America? Is this a compelling lens through which to view *Gatsby*? Why or why not? *Use evidence from Roberts and* Gatsby *in your response.*

May be photocopied for classroom use. *Using Informational Text to Teach* The Great Gatsby by Audrey Fisch and Susan Chenelle © 2018 (Lanham, MD: Rowman & Littlefield).

E. What is the significance of the people on the margins in *Gatsby*?

1. **Discuss**: Although Gatsby is a novel concerned with the lives of wealthy white people, it is also populated along the margins with characters who are specifically identified as different in terms of race, ethnicity, and class. Consider both the marginal characters who appear briefly within the novel and the secondary characters. How are these characters represented and identified? What sort of language is used to describe them? What do they add to the novel? Why, especially for the marginal characters, do you think Fitzgerald includes them and chooses to describe and identify them as he does? How does attention to them and to their race, ethnic, or class identity add to your understanding of the world of white privilege at the center of *Gatsby*? *Use Table 2.8 to record your analysis.*

2. **Discuss**: Consider the ways in which Stoddard and Roberts would describe and discuss the characters you have analyzed above. Would they consider these characters white? Would they consider them a threat to white civilization? Why or why not? *Use Table 2.9 to record your analysis.*

3. **Write**: Pick two or three of the characters you have discussed. Who are these people? How do they operate in relation to or on the margins of the world of white privilege in *Gatsby*? What do they reveal about the wealthy white world at the center in *Gatsby*? Do they represent a threat to that world and to white civilization? What do you think Fitzgerald hopes to accomplish by including these characters in his novel? *Use evidence from Stoddard, Roberts, and* Gatsby *in your response.*

Tables are available for download at http://www.usinginformationaltext.com/student.

CLASS ACTIVITY

Task: Your goal is to write a treatment for the use of the cover image of Stoddard's *The Rising Tide of Color Against White World-Supremacy* along with any accompanying music or sound effects in a new film version of *Gatsby*.

In groups:

1. **Review the different cover images for Stoddard's volume and select the one you think best suits a new film version of *Gatsby*.** Think about whether you would use the same cover image for Tom's copy of *The Rising Tide of Color Against White World-Supremacy* as for Gatsby's copy of Stoddard's work. Write a brief argument explaining your choices.

2. **Discuss**: How will you use this image of the Stoddard cover in your film? For example, will you simply have the book on display on a coffee table in the New York City apartment in chapter 2? Will you use the cover art more dramatically at this or any other moment in the film?

3. **Discuss**: Will you use any particular music or sound effects to underscore the issues of race raised by Tom and delineated in texts such as *The Rising Tide of Color Against White World-Supremacy* and *Why Europe Leaves Home*? When and how will you use music or sound effects here?

As a class:

4. **Discuss or debate**: Each group shares its plans and rationale for the use of the cover image and any music or sound effects. Which plans are most persuasive and compelling? Why?

May be photocopied for classroom use. *Using Informational Text to Teach* The Great Gatsby by Audrey Fisch and Susan Chenelle © 2018 (Lanham, MD: Rowman & Littlefield).

Individually:

5. **Write your treatment and reflection.**

Part 1: Write your treatment for your film version of *Gatsby*, with a specific focus on which cover(s) of *The Rising Tide of Color Against White World-Supremacy* you plan to include and how you plan to incorporate the image(s) in your film. Discuss as well your plans for the inclusion of music or sound effects.

Part 2: Make an argument about why your treatment best reflects your understanding of Stoddard's ideas and their relevance to *Gatsby*. Be sure to explain how your choices reflect Tom's views about "civilization" as evidenced in *Gatsby* and as reflective of ideas about white supremacy circulating broadly in the world of *Gatsby*. Use textual evidence from Stoddard, Roberts, and *Gatsby* together with careful analysis of the visual imagery in the cover and of your musical selections to make your argument.

Part 3: Write a reflection in which you explain how your ideas for your treatment evolved as a result of the group and whole-class discussion. Did your choices change? Why? How did your peers' ideas influence your thinking?

CLASS ACTIVITY RUBRIC

Category	4—Excellent	3—Good	2—Satisfactory	1—Unsatisfactory
Treatment (integration of knowledge and ideas)	Treatment shows outstanding understanding of Stoddard's ideas and the role of racism and white supremacy in *Gatsby* as a whole	Treatment shows good understanding of Stoddard's ideas and the role of racism and white supremacy in *Gatsby* as a whole	Treatment shows limited or uneven understanding of Stoddard's ideas and the role of racism and white supremacy in *Gatsby* as a whole	Treatment shows insufficient or inaccurate understanding of Stoddard's ideas and the role of racism and white supremacy in *Gatsby* as a whole
Discussion and debate (participate in a range of conversations; present information, findings, and supporting evidence)	Outstanding participation in small-group and whole-class discussions, showing an outstanding ability to listen and contribute to collaborative discussions	Good participation in small-group and whole-class discussions, showing a good ability to listen and contribute to collaborative discussions	Limited or uneven participation in small-group and whole-class discussions, showing a limited or uneven ability to listen and contribute to collaborative discussions	Insufficient or unsuccessful participation in small-group and whole-class discussions, showing an emerging but insufficient ability to listen and contribute to collaborative discussions
Individual reflection (cite relevant and sufficient textual evidence; improve writing and argumentation through reflection)	Reflection is clear, coherent, and shows excellent insight into the texts; reflection is outstanding and well informed by small-group and whole-class discussion	Reflection is solid and shows good insight into the texts; reflection is thoughtful and informed by small-group and whole-class discussion	Reflection is limited or uneven and shows limited insight into the texts; reflection is limited and unevenly informed by small-group and whole-class discussion	Reflection is unclear and/or incoherent and shows little insight into the texts; reflection is incoherent and not clearly informed by small-group and whole-class discussion
Vocabulary (use domain-specific vocabulary)	Several "words to own" from the unit are used correctly in treatment and/or reflection	Some "words to own" from the unit are used correctly in treatment and/or reflection	One or more "words to own" from the unit are used but perhaps not correctly or effectively in treatment and/or reflection	No "words to own" from the unit are used in treatment and/or reflection

May be photocopied for classroom use. *Using Informational Text to Teach* The Great Gatsby by Audrey Fisch and Susan Chenelle © 2018 (Lanham, MD: Rowman & Littlefield).

Category	4—Excellent	3—Good	2—Satisfactory	1—Unsatisfactory
Documentation and style (in-text citation and works cited)	Treatment and reflection conform to the appropriate style guidelines (MLA) for in-text citation and works cited	Treatment and reflection conform with limited errors to the appropriate style guidelines (MLA) for in-text citation and works cited	Treatment and reflection attempt to conform to the appropriate style guidelines (MLA) for in-text citation and works cited but do so ineffectively or inaccurately	Treatment and reflection do not conform to the appropriate style guidelines (MLA) for in-text citation and works cited

UNIT 3

Does Money Make People Such as Tom Mean?

TEACHER'S GUIDE

Overview

This section draws on our sense that *Gatsby* offers students an important opportunity to reflect on cheating, entitlement, dominance, and incivility. All of these issues have, unfortunately, echoes in our broader society and in many of our schools. Bad behavior, including bullying and cheating, is all too common.

Moreover, we sometimes hear, in both individual and public discourse, a slippery and suspicious rhetoric in which the cheater or bully justifies his or her behavior, with a rhetoric underscored by a sense that the normal rules of society somehow don't apply to him or her. Unfortunately, Fitzgerald's description of "careless people" who wreak havoc—"they smashed up things and creatures and then retreated back into their money or their vast carelessness"—continues to resonate today.

University of California-Irvine researcher Paul Piff offers students an intriguing entrance into these issues through social science research. He describes, in the excerpts from a TED Talk transcript we include below, a series of experiments designed to explore the ways in which money and privilege may increase individual bad behavior. The ideas in this section help students move beyond a focus on individual bad actors, such as Tom, and the broader social and psychological forces that may drive certain kinds of behaviors.

Of particular interest in the selection from Piff is his focus on how social science research also can be used to produce good outcomes: greater empathy, for example, can be produced through small interventions. Given that *Gatsby* is such a bleak text, and one in which heroism and role models are in short supply and broader morality doesn't seem to play any part, Piff's discussion about how researchers, wealthy individuals, and activists are working to combat the meanness augmented by economic and social inequality is heartening.

Timing

Meanness pervades *Gatsby*, and teachers may want to introduce this text at any time during the reading of the novel to allow students to place the bad behavior in the text within the interesting context of social science provided by Paul Piff. However, the text could also be fruitfully introduced in connection with chapter 2, in which Tom strikingly displays his dominance and meanness in relation to those around him. Obviously, waiting until students have completed all of *Gatsby* allows students to connect Piff's text more broadly to the ways in which Tom and Daisy feel entitled to cheat and operate outside the traditional boundaries and laws of civil society.

Consider the following guidelines regarding when to undertake the different activities:

Essential Question for Discussion and Writing	Objective	Suggested Timing	Suggested Rubric	Additional Research
A. What do the experiments show? RI 1, 2, 3, 4, 5, 6, 8, 10 W 1, 2, 4, 5, 9, 10 SL 1, 4 L 1, 2, 3, 5, 6	SW analyze the transcript from Paul Piff's TED Talk and explore the findings of his research at Berkeley about the relationship between wealth and money on the one hand and entitlement, greed, and meanness on the other hand.	Any time—this set of questions doesn't require any knowledge of *Gatsby*.	A	N

Essential Question for Discussion and Writing	Objective	Suggested Timing	Suggested Rubric	Additional Research
B. Does money make Tom mean? RL 1, 2, 3, 4, 5, 9, 10 RI 1, 2, 3, 4, 5, 6, 8, 9, 10 W 1, 2, 4, 5, 9, 10 SL 1, 4 L 1, 2, 3, 5, 6	SW apply the findings of Piff's experiments in order to consider whether Tom's behavior correlates with Piff's theory that money makes people mean.	Any time or after chapter 2 (when we encounter Tom's entitlement and brutality)	A	N
C. Is it every man (or woman) for himself (or herself)? RL 1, 2, 3, 4, 5, 6, 9, 10 RI 1, 2, 3, 4, 5, 8, 9, 10 W 1, 2, 4, 5, 9, 10 SL 1, 4 L 1, 2, 3, 5, 6	SW explore how the behavior of the characters in *Gatsby* does or does not conform to Piff's ideas that, in a climate of economic inequality, the wealthy are more likely to pursue personal success at the expense of others.	After chapter 6 (when we learn about how Gatsby has made his money) or after chapter 8 (when Gatsby's fall is completed by his death)	A	N
Class Activity				
Using Piff's ideas, transform chapter 2 in order to feature a Monopoly game among the characters in the novel. RL 1, 2, 3, 4, 5, 6, 9, 10 RI 1, 2, 3, 4, 5, 9, 10 W 1, 2, 3, 4, 5, 9, 10 SL 1, 4 L 1, 2, 3, 5, 6	SW use their understanding of Piff's experiments to rewrite chapter 2 to feature a Monopoly game; they will also perform their new chapters and reflect on the performances in order to consider whether, as Piff suggests, money makes people such as Tom mean.	This activity might be completed after students finish chapter 2 or any time after.	Rubric included	N

NOTES ON THE READINGS

- The fact that this reading draws on social science experiments means teachers may want to think about opportunities for cross-disciplinary collaboration with colleagues in other content areas. Science or social studies teachers, for example, might engage students in discussion of the particular challenges of social science research involving experiments with human behavior. Students can be encouraged to think about the ways in which Piff's experiments involve collecting different kinds of data. The Monopoly game, for example, required qualitative analysis of players' behavior, whereas the analysis of drivers' behavior was based on quantitative data.
- Meanness, of the kind Piff considers, is not limited to the wealthy characters in *Gatsby*. At the same time, most of the primary characters in *Gatsby* are wealthy, so students will need to think hard about examples from among the minor characters of people who are not mean. The question of whether Gatsby himself reflects or negates Piff's thesis should also prove engaging for students.

SUGGESTED MEDIA LINKS

- Students are likely to be fascinated to learn the history of the now ubiquitous game of Monopoly, including the fact that it was invented by Quaker Elizabeth Magie as "The Landlord's Game" in order to teach about the danger of greed. The Smithsonian channel on YouTube has a great five-minute video on "The Landlord's Game," with a focus on Magie's anticapitalist agenda and the rejection of her game by the game makers Parker Brothers.
- Students might be equally intrigued by people trying to use the game today, with different rules than those employed by Piff, in order to teach about housing discrimination and the inequalities of home ownership. See, for example, St. Louis University Professor Richard Harvey, who designed "Intergroup Monopoly" to explore systemic, group-based inequalities and the difficulties of overcoming these for his class, "The Psychology of Oppression." Students could easily and quickly play by Harvey's rules, which are freely available for public use on the Web, as a counterpoint to Piff's experiments.
- A very brief animated video, "What Is Social Science," from the UK's Economic and Social Science Research Council does a fantastic job of introducing students to the notion of social science research, including discussion of the kinds of questions social science researchers ask, the ways they go about conducting research, the concept of peer review, and some of the ways in which society has benefited from social science research.

- Also useful is a two-minute YouTube segment featuring economist Milton Friedman speaking with Phil Donohue in an impassioned defense of free enterprise and greed. Students will find the clothing and hairstyles dated, but they likely will find compelling the contrast between Donohue's concerns about inequality and injustice on the one hand and Friedman's dispassionate defense on the other hand of greed and individuals pursuing their self-interest.
- Students are often taught that bullies operate from a position of insecurity and weakness. Piff's research suggests the opposite: those in power in situations of inequality exhibit "meanness." Teachers may want to work with some of the local anti-bullying materials in their school and district to think through this issue.

VOCABULARY WARM-UP

WORDS TO OWN: attuned, concentrated, demonstrative, detriment, dominance, egalitarian, empathy, entitlement, hierarchical, ideology, inevitably, innate, malleable, material, moralize, privileged

Section A: Use context clues: Read the following sentences and use context clues to determine the meaning of the italicized words.

1. Piff uses a game of Monopoly to understand "society and its *hierarchical* structure, wherein some people have a lot of wealth and a lot of status, and a lot of people don't." He is interested in "the effects of these kinds of *hierarchies*." There are many *hierarchies* in the world, but what Piff is interested in is the systemic ranking of people in relation to wealth. What other kinds of *hierarchies* exist in American society? Beyond wealth, how else are people in our society ranked? What *hierarchies* exist in your school?

2. As young people think ahead, one of the biggest decisions they face is how to balance the quest for *material* success with the desire for meaning in life. If you love playing the guitar, are you willing to pursue that as a career even if it means less *material* success? Or do you think that money and financial security are the most important consideration as you plan your future? Why do you think some people place so much value on *material* success? Do you? Why?

3. Piff writes that some people are more likely to "*moralize* greed being good." In general, we think of greed as a bad quality. Why would some people try to *moralize* the opposite: that greed is good? What do you think it means to *moralize* something? Do you see any relationship between morals and *moralizing*? Would you characterize those who *moralize* that greed is good as being moral? Why or why not?

May be photocopied for classroom use. *Using Informational Text to Teach* The Great Gatsby by Audrey Fisch and Susan Chenelle © 2018 (Lanham, MD: Rowman & Littlefield).

4. Do you think generosity is an *innate* character trait or characteristic that one is born with, or do you think a person can change and become more generous? If personal qualities, such as generosity toward others, are not *innate*, where do they come from? What do you think determines whether one is generous toward others?

5. Tail wagging can be a sign of friendliness in a dog, but it can also be a signal of *dominance* in which the animal uses its tail to indicate that it is the boss of another dog. Humans use a variety of signs to indicate *dominance* over one another. How do the big dogs at your school exhibit *dominance* over others?

6. It can be difficult for the president to stay *attuned* to the realities of everyday life in the United States. Because presidents don't shop for groceries, drive a car or commute to work, cook food, or take care of a home, they can find themselves out of touch with ordinary Americans. If you were a world leader, how would you try to keep yourself *attuned* to the ordinary world?

7. Research suggests that, contrary to popular belief, intelligence is not an *innate* quality; rather, intelligence is *malleable*, something you can improve with time and effort. Why do you think we tend to think of intelligence as *innate*? If you recognized that intelligence is instead *malleable*, would that change how you think about your own ability and potential? Why?

Section B: More context clues: Here your task is to use context clues to understand the italicized word's meaning AND to practice your context clues skills.

1. Piff writes that his experiments reveal "that as a person's levels of wealth increase, their feelings of compassion and *empathy* go down." *Empathy* can best be defined as

    a) the ability to read minds
    b) power
    c) creativity
    d) sympathy for others

2. Which word(s) from the sentence in Question 1 best helps the reader understand the meaning of *empathy*?

   a) compassion
   b) feelings
   c) levels of wealth
   d) go down

3. One version of the American Dream is the idea that "sometimes, you need to put your own interests above the interests and well-being of other people around you . . . to pursue a vision of personal success, of achievement and accomplishment, to the *detriment* of others around you." In this sentence, *detriment* most closely means

   a) disadvantage
   b) determination
   c) competition
   d) improvement

4. Which word(s) from the sentence in Question 3 best helps the reader understand the meaning of *detriment*?

   a) above the well-being of other people
   b) pursue
   c) others around you
   d) a vision of personal success

5. We are the One Percent, the Resource Generation, and Wealth for Common Good are organizations in which "the most privileged members of the population, people who are wealthy, are using their own economic resources, to combat inequality by advocating for social policies, changes in social values, and changes in people's behavior, that work against their own economic interests but that may ultimately restore the American Dream." Based on the context, you can understand *privileged* to mean

   a) fancy
   b) generous
   c) rich
   d) liberal

6. Which word(s) from the sentences in Question 5 best help you understand the meaning of *privileged*?

   a) people who are wealthy
   b) Common Good
   c) restore the American Dream
   d) to combat inequality

Section C: Sometimes common words are used in uncommon ways. **Use the dictionary** in order to understand the uncommon meanings of the italicized common words.

1. Piff notes that in his experiments "the rich players actually started to become ruder toward the other person, less and less sensitive to the plight of those poor, poor players, and more and more demonstrative of their *material* success." Piff isn't talking about how the rich players dressed or the *material* they wore, so what does he mean when he says they flaunted their "*material* success"?

2. What is the relationship between those who *moralize* and morals? Is it necessarily good or bad to *moralize*?

3. If wealth is "becoming increasingly *concentrated* in the hands of a select group of individuals," what does that mean? *Concentrated* detergent is intense and extra powerful; you can use a small amount to wash a large amount of clothing. Is *concentrated* wealth similar or different? If wealth is becoming *concentrated*, what does that mean? Why might *concentrated* wealth be bad?

Section D: Use the dictionary to look up the italicized words and answer the following questions based on their definitions.

1. For a long time, cigarette companies hid the fact that smoking was *detrimental* to people's health. In fact, some advertising suggested that smoking was healthy. Are there products on the market today that you suspect may be a *detriment* to those who use them? Which products and why?

2. Do you consider yourself an *egalitarian* person? If yes, why do you think this is an *ideology* that makes sense? If no, why do you think *egalitarianism* is not a useful set of beliefs with which to view the world? Explain.

3. Some people are more *attuned* than others to the world around them. Are you naturally *attuned* to others? Can you sit by and ignore another student's distress? Or do you feel the need to offer support? Is being *attuned* to the needs and feelings of those around you a blessing or a curse? Explain your thinking.

4. Do you want a romantic partner who is openly *demonstrative* in his or her affection toward you, or do you think public displays of affection are inappropriate and unwelcome? Explain your thinking about whether or not you think a *demonstrative* partner is appealing.

5. Do you believe in fate or the idea that our future is already mapped out for us and *inevitable*? Have you ever felt as if you were destined to end up in a certain place or with a certain result, *inevitably*, no matter how much you tried to change course? Explain whether you think much of your life is *inevitable* or whether you think you have the power to determine your future.

6. Some people worry that the millennial generation has developed an unhealthy sense of *entitlement*. Also known as the trophy generation, millennials were often raised in a culture of praise in which their smallest achievements were rewarded with approval and trophies. As a result, some millennials think that simple participation, rather than real achievement as a result of hard work, is sufficient and *entitles* them to unearned rewards and advancement. What do you think about this argument? Were you raised this way? Do you think positive reinforcement and a culture of praise can result in an unhealthy sense of *entitlement* that stifles hard work?

7. Do you think *empathy* is an important life skill? Why or why not? Should schools try to help students develop *empathy*? If yes, how do you think they should go about that? If no, why not?

Section E: Practice using the word correctly by choosing the correct form of the word(s) that best fits in the blank within the following sentences.

1. Race is the classification, often as a _____, of people based on skin color, hair texture, and other physical characteristics. Many argue that this kind of arbitrary categorization of people lends itself to a _____ and unequal society.

   a) hierarchical . . . hierarchy
   b) hierarchy . . . hierarchical
   c) hierarchy . . . hierarchy
   d) hierarchical . . . hierarchical

2. Researchers were surprised to see that giving one player an unfair advantage in a game of Monopoly _____ produced bad behavior in that player; the study suggests that meanness may be an _____ result of wealth.

   a) inevitable . . . inevitable
   b) inevitably . . . inevitably
   c) inevitable . . . inevitably
   d) inevitably . . . inevitable

3. I want to work in an _____ workplace; I think _____ represents both an important ideology and a sound business practice.

   a) egalitarian . . . egalitarianism
   b) egalitarianism . . . egalitarian
   c) egalitarian . . . egalitarian
   d) egalitarianism . . . egalitarianism

4. At this historical moment, much of the wealth in the United States is _____ among a very small percentage of the population. This _____ of wealth poses a fundamental challenge to the American Dream and the ideology of fairness and equality.

   a) concentrated . . . concentrate
   b) concentrate . . . concentration
   c) concentration . . . concentrate
   d) concentrated . . . concentration

5. In debates, politicians often try to ____ their opponents by shouting over them; do you find these shows of ____ amusing or depressing?

   a) dominate . . . dominance
   b) dominance . . . dominate
   c) dominate . . . dominate
   d) dominance . . . dominance

Section F: Vocabulary skits

Use the model sentences and definitions to understand the words in question. Create a skit in which you address the given topic. Every member of the group must use the vocabulary word at least once during your performance of the skit.

1. *entitlement*—the belief that one deserves special treatment or privileges, the idea that one has a special claim to certain rights

   - Politicians often complain about *entitlements*, but many *entitlement* programs, such as social security, are highly valued in our society for providing important benefits to those, such as the elderly, who have earned special benefits.
   - Do you think that waiters should be *entitled* to earn a minimum wage salary, or does the fact that they also earn tips mean that they do not deserve the same wage *entitlement* as other types of workers?
   - The soccer team has begun to behave like *entitled* brats; just because they won the state championship does not mean that they should be exempt from regular school rules, such as wearing their uniforms and coming to school on time. Their *entitlement* is so offensive!

Scenario: Create a skit in which a group of student journalists discuss what they see as an attitude of *entitlement* among the newest members of the school newspaper. What sorts of privileges are the new reporters asking for? Why do the more senior reporters find this kind of *entitlement* from the newer journalists offensive or inappropriate? New reporters might talk about expecting to get to write whatever stories they want. Senior journalists might talk about how when they started on the newspaper, no one dared to be so *entitled* about what stories they got to write, and so forth.

2. *ideology*—a set of beliefs about people and culture, sometimes particular to a specific group or political organization

   - A feminist *ideology* is a set of beliefs about the ways in which gender equality is central to making the world a better place.
   - Politicians often claim that they are driven by commonsense solutions to problems, rather than *ideology*, but one might argue that the way in which we see even an ordinary problem is shaped in part by the larger religious, political, or social *ideology* we have about the world.
   - Her actions stem from an underlying humanitarian *ideology*; she thinks that each of us has a responsibility to look out for the less fortunate among us.

Scenario: Thanksgiving is a holiday of food and fun, but it also a time when families get together and talk politics. You are a family seated around the dinner table at Thanksgiving, and the conversation turns to politics. Some family members lean to the left, and others reflect a right-wing *ideology*. How does the conversation go? Is the family able to make peace despite their *ideological* differences? Or do some family members need to flee the holiday meal? Is there a particular family member who tries to hold everyone together at the table despite the different political *ideologies*?

3. *malleable*—able to be shaped or changed by outside influences or others, not rigid or inflexible

   - I try to be *malleable* in my views; the world is a complex place, and I can't begin to understand how everything works.
   - My sister can be too *malleable* in her opinions; if her friend offers an opinion about a song or a movie, my sister immediately adopts that view. She has no mind of her own!
   - Do you think your values are fixed or *malleable*; are you open to suggestion or set in your views?

Scenario: Create a skit in which a group of advertising executives discusses how to create enthusiasm for a new flavor of chips: broccoli-flavored chips! As part of the planning, the executives discuss how *malleable* people's chip preferences are. Can they get people to try the new flavor? How can they make people more *malleable* in relation to broccoli-flavored chips? How might they approach their advertising campaign in order to make broccoli-flavored chips a success?

May be photocopied for classroom use. *Using Informational Text to Teach* The Great Gatsby by Audrey Fisch and Susan Chenelle © 2018 (Lanham, MD: Rowman & Littlefield).

ESSENTIAL QUESTION: DOES MONEY MAKE PEOPLE SUCH AS TOM MEAN?

Introduction

In this unit, we read a piece of social psychology in order to think about the broader context for some of the less-than-nice behaviors we see in *Gatsby*. How are Fitzgerald's characters and their actions shaped by their class backgrounds? What social and psychological forces contribute to making them into who they are and how they behave toward others? Paul Piff, a professor of psychology and social behavior, studies how personal behavior is shaped by the advantages and disadvantages of wealth and social class.

In this reading, excerpted from a TED Talk transcript, he explores the idea that money makes people mean. Piff discusses the experiments he conducted and what they reveal about how wealth breeds greed, a diminution of empathy and compassion, and unethical behavior. Piff also explores the implications of his findings, particularly given current levels of inequality in the United States, for the future of the American Dream.

From "Does money make you mean?" by Paul Piff

I want you to, for a moment, think about playing a game of Monopoly, except in this game, that combination of skill, talent and luck that help earn you success in games, as in life, has been rendered irrelevant, because this game's been rigged, and you've got the upper hand. You've got more money, more opportunities to move around the board, and more access to

---

Reflect on the essential question: Do you think money can change people's behavior toward others? Can having money make someone mean? Do you think researchers would be able to study and answer this question?

Reflect on the introduction: Based on what you have read in the introduction, what do you know about what Paul Piff studies? What kind of an audience do you think Piff is speaking to in his TED Talk? How might his presentation of his research here be different from a publication in a scholarly journal? Are you surprised by the idea offered in the introduction that wealth breeds greed?

Reflect on the title: Do you think Piff will be able to answer this question convincingly? What answer do you expect? What do you think about this question?

Reflect on the opening paragraph: What skills are normally necessary to win a game of Monopoly? How is the "rigged game" of Monopoly Piff is describing different? What connection is Piff suggesting between Monopoly and life?

May be photocopied for classroom use. *Using Informational Text to Teach* The Great Gatsby by Audrey Fisch and Susan Chenelle © 2018 (Lanham, MD: Rowman & Littlefield).

resources. And as you think about that experience, I want you to ask yourself, how might that experience of being a *privileged* player in a rigged game change the way that you think about yourself and regard that other player?

So we ran a study on the U.C. Berkeley campus to look at exactly that question. We brought in more than 100 pairs of strangers into the lab, and with the flip of a coin randomly assigned one of the two to be a rich player in a rigged game. They got two times as much money. When they passed Go, they collected twice the salary, and they got to roll both dice instead of one, so they got to move around the board a lot more. And over the course of 15 minutes, we watched through hidden cameras what happened.

Rich Player: How many 500s did you have?

Poor Player: Just one.

Rich Player: Are you serious.

Poor Player: Yeah.

Rich Player: I have three. (Laughs) I don't know why they gave me so much.

Paul Piff: Okay, so it was quickly apparent to players that something was up. One person clearly has a lot more money than the other person, and yet, as the game unfolded, we saw very notable differences and dramatic differences begin to emerge between the two players. The rich player started to move around the board louder, literally smacking the board with his/her piece as he/she went around. We were more likely to see signs of *dominance* and nonverbal signs, displays of power and celebration among the rich players.

We had a bowl of pretzels positioned off to the side. . . . That allowed us to watch

Key idea: How exactly were the games rigged at Berkeley? What do you think the researchers were trying to study?

Reflect on the dialogue between the Rich Player and the Poor Player: What does the dialogue reveal about what they understand about the experiment? Do they know the game is rigged?

Key idea: Why does Piff discuss the Rich Player's movement of his piece around the Monopoly board? What is important about the Rich Player's behavior?

Vocabulary: Piff notes that the researchers saw signs of dominance from the rich players. Put this into your own words. Why do you think the researchers saw these signs of dominance as important?

Key idea: The researchers place a bowl of pretzels near the game players to study their consumption of pretzels or their consummatory behavior. Why? What do they discover? How did the rich player's consummatory behavior differ from the poor player's consummatory behavior? What conclusions do the researchers draw about the players' consumption of the pretzels?

May be photocopied for classroom use. *Using Informational Text to Teach* The Great Gatsby by Audrey Fisch and Susan Chenelle © 2018 (Lanham, MD: Rowman & Littlefield). Excerpts from "Does money make you mean?" by Paul Piff. TEDxMarin. Reprinted with permission. All rights reserved.

participants' consummatory behavior. So we're just tracking how many pretzels participants eat.

Rich Player: Are those pretzels a trick?

Poor Player: I don't know.

Piff: Okay, so no surprises, people are onto us. They wonder what that bowl of pretzels is doing there in the first place. One even asks, like you just saw, is that bowl of pretzels there as a trick? And yet, despite that, the power of the situation seems to *inevitably dominate*, and those rich players start to eat more pretzels.

Rich Player: I love pretzels.

Piff: And as the game went on, one of the really interesting and dramatic patterns that we observed begin to emerge was that the rich players actually started to become ruder toward the other person, less and less sensitive to the plight of those poor, poor players, and more and more *demonstrative* of their *material* success, more likely to showcase how well they're doing.

Rich Player: I have money for everything.

Poor Player: How much is that?

Rich Player: You owe me $24. You're going to lose all your money soon. I'll buy it. I have so much money. I have so much money, it takes me forever.

Rich Player 2: I'm going to buy out this whole board.

Rich Player 3: You're going to run out of money soon. I'm pretty much untouchable at this point.

Piff: Okay, and here's what I think was really, really interesting, is that at the end of the 15 minutes, we asked the players to talk about their experience during the game. And when the rich players talked about why they had inevitably won in this rigged game of Monopoly—they talked about what they'd done to buy those different properties and earn their success in the game, and they became far less *attuned* to all those

> **Key idea:** What does Piff mean when he says "the power of the situation seems to inevitably dominate"? State this idea in your own words.
>
> **Key idea:** Piff claims that the rich players became "ruder." What evidence does he offer for this assertion? Why is this rudeness surprising? What does Piff see as significant to the experiment about this rudeness?
>
> **Key idea:** After playing the rigged game, players talked about why they had won. What does Piff discover about how the richer players viewed their success? What does Piff mean when he references the "incredible insight into how the mind makes sense of advantage"? How do the rich players in this experiment make sense of their advantage?

May be photocopied for classroom use. *Using Informational Text to Teach* The Great Gatsby by Audrey Fisch and Susan Chenelle © 2018 (Lanham, MD: Rowman & Littlefield). Excerpts from "Does money make you mean?" by Paul Piff. TEDxMarin. Reprinted with permission. All rights reserved.

different features of the situation, including that flip of a coin that had randomly gotten them into that privileged position in the first place. And that's a really, really incredible insight into how the mind makes sense of advantage.

Now this game of Monopoly can be used as a metaphor for understanding society and its *hierarchical* structure, wherein some people have a lot of wealth and a lot of status, and a lot of people don't. They have a lot less wealth and a lot less status and a lot less access to valued resources. And what my colleagues and I for the last seven years have been doing is studying the effects of these kinds of *hierarchies*. What we've been finding across dozens of studies and thousands of participants across this country is that as a person's level of wealth increases, their feelings of compassion and *empathy* go down, and their feelings of *entitlement*, of deservingness, and their *ideology* of self-interest increases. In surveys, we found that it's actually wealthier individuals who are more likely to *moralize* greed being good, and that the pursuit of self-interest is favorable and moral. Now what I want to do today is talk about some of the implications of this *ideology* of self-interest, talk about why we should care about those implications, and end with what might be done.

> **Vocabulary:** Piff references society's "hierarchical structure." What does he mean? How is society hierarchical?
>
> **Key idea:** Piff writes that "as a person's level of wealth increases, their feelings of compassion and empathy go down, and their feelings of entitlement, of deservingness, and their ideology of self-interest increases." Put this into your own words.
>
> **Key idea:** What do you think it means to "moralize greed being good"?
>
> **Reflect:** What connection is Piff suggesting between the rich players' behavior in the rigged Monopoly game and this ideology of self-interest?
>
> **Key idea:** What finding does the candy jar experiment produce? Why is the finding important to the overall study of wealth and behavior?

We ran another study where we looked at whether people would be inclined to take candy from a jar of candy that we explicitly identified as being reserved for children. We explicitly told participants this jar of candy is for children participating in a developmental lab nearby. They're in studies. This is for them. And we just monitored how much candy participants took. Participants who felt rich took two times as much candy as participants who felt poor.

May be photocopied for classroom use. *Using Informational Text to Teach* The Great Gatsby by Audrey Fisch and Susan Chenelle © 2018 (Lanham, MD: Rowman & Littlefield). Excerpts from "Does money make you mean?" by Paul Piff. TEDxMarin. Reprinted with permission. All rights reserved.

We've even studied cars, not just any cars, but whether drivers of different kinds of cars are more or less inclined to break the law. In one of these studies, we looked at whether drivers would stop for a pedestrian that we had posed waiting to cross at a crosswalk. . . . What we found was that as the expensiveness of a car increased, the driver's tendencies to break the law increased as well. None of the cars, none of the cars in our least expensive car category broke the law. Close to 50 percent of the cars in our most expensive vehicle category broke the law.

[T]he American Dream is an idea in which we all have an equal opportunity to succeed and prosper, as long as we apply ourselves and work hard, and a piece of that means that sometimes, you need to put your own interests above the interests and well-being of other people around you. But what we're finding is that, the wealthier you are, the more likely you are to pursue a vision of personal success, of achievement and accomplishment, to the *detriment* of others around you.

> **Key idea:** What finding does the driving experiment produce? Why were researchers interested in the behavior of those who drove expensive cars versus those who drove inexpensive cars? Why is the finding important to the overall study of wealth and behavior?
>
> **Key idea:** What point is Piff making about self-interest and the American Dream? What effect, according to his research, does wealth have on the American Dream?

[Piff then turns to the gap or difference between the mean or average household income for those at the bottom and those at the top of American society.]

[O]ver the last 20 years, that significant difference [in average income] has become a grand canyon of sorts between those at the top and everyone else. In fact, the top 20 percent of our population own close to 90 percent of the total wealth in this country. We're at unprecedented levels of economic inequality. What that means is that wealth is not only becoming increasingly *concentrated* in the hands of a select group of individuals, but the American Dream is becoming increasingly

> **Reflect:** Why does Piff describe the income gap in American society as a "grand canyon"? Has this gap always been a canyon? What connection is Piff making between the income gap and the behavior of his rich players or the entitled expensive car drivers?

May be photocopied for classroom use. *Using Informational Text to Teach* The Great Gatsby by Audrey Fisch and Susan Chenelle © 2018 (Lanham, MD: Rowman & Littlefield). Excerpts from "Does money make you mean?" by Paul Piff. TEDxMarin. Reprinted with permission. All rights reserved.

unattainable for an increasing majority of us. And if it's the case, as we've been finding, that the wealthier you are, the more entitled you feel to that wealth, and the more likely you are to prioritize your own interests above the interests of other people, and be willing to do things to serve that self-interest, well then there's no reason to think that those patterns will change. So what do we do?

[W]e've been finding in our own laboratory research that small psychological interventions, small changes to people's values, small nudges in certain directions, can restore levels of *egalitarianism* and *empathy*. In one study, we had people watch a brief video, just 46 seconds long, about childhood poverty that served as a reminder of the needs of others in the world around them, and after watching that, we looked at how willing people were to offer up their own time to a stranger presented to them in the lab who was in distress. After watching this video, an hour later, rich people became just as generous of their own time to help out this other person, a stranger, as someone who's poor, suggesting that these differences are not *innate* or categorical, but are so *malleable* to slight changes in people's values, and little nudges of compassion and bumps of empathy.

And beyond the walls of our lab, we're even beginning to see signs of change in society. Bill Gates, one of our nation's wealthiest individuals, in his Harvard commencement speech, talked about . . . inequality as being the most daunting challenge, and talked

Key idea: Piff indicates that the wealthy "are more likely" to "be willing to do things" to serve their own "self-interest." How does this self-interestedness connect back to the mean behavior of the rich players in the Monopoly game, the pretzel-eating of the rich players, or the driving behavior of those with expensive cars? Why is Piff worried about the American Dream?

Key idea: What is the purpose of the video experiment? What did researchers discover from the experiment?

Vocabulary: Piff indicates that differences in generosity toward others are not "innate" but are "malleable." Put this into your words. Are you surprised by this idea?

Reflect: The selection closes with a discussion of the work of Bill Gates and other privileged members of the population. Why does Piff end with a discussion of the work of the rich? How does this discussion connect with Piff's initial question, "Does money make you mean?"

May be photocopied for classroom use. *Using Informational Text to Teach* The Great Gatsby by Audrey Fisch and Susan Chenelle © 2018 (Lanham, MD: Rowman & Littlefield). Excerpts from "Does money make you mean?" by Paul Piff. TEDxMarin. Reprinted with permission. All rights reserved.

about what must be done to combat it, saying, "Humanity's greatest advances are not in its discoveries, but in how those discoveries are applied to reduce inequity."

. . . And there's the emergence of dozens of grassroots movements, like We are the One Percent, the Resource Generation, or Wealth for Common Good, in which the most privileged members of the population, people who are wealthy, are using their own economic resources to combat inequality by advocating for social policies, changes in social values, and changes in people's behavior, that work against their own economic interests but that may ultimately restore the American Dream.

Piff, Paul. "Does Money Make You Mean?" TED, December 2013, www.ted.com/talks/paul_piff_does_money_make_you_mean/transcript?language=en.

CHECK FOR UNDERSTANDING

1. In the first experiment at Berkeley that Piff discusses, pairs of strangers played Monopoly. Why does Piff refer to the players as "Poor Player" and "Rich Player"?

   a) The "Rich Players" were the ones who won the games.
   b) The "Poor Players" were the ones who lost the games.
   c) The game was rigged so that one player in each pair was given more money.
   d) Some of the players were not very skilled at playing Monopoly.

2. What is the central idea of Piff's remarks?

   a) Many people in the world are willing to cheat in order to get ahead.
   b) Rich people are less kind than poor people.
   c) Inequality can lead to greed and entitlement, but people can also be encouraged to be more compassionate.
   d) The American Dream is in danger.

3. Which THREE sentences from the text best support the answer to the question above?

   a) "[T]he American Dream is becoming increasingly unattainable for an increasing majority of us."
   b) "Participants who felt rich took two times as much candy as participants who felt poor."
   c) "[S]mall changes to people's values, small nudges in certain directions, can restore levels of egalitarianism and empathy."
   d) "They have a lot less wealth and a lot less status and a lot less access to valued resources."
   e) "[W]e found that it's actually wealthier individuals who are more likely to moralize greed being good, and that the pursuit of self-interest is favorable and moral."
   f) "[T]he American Dream is an idea in which we all have an equal opportunity to succeed and prosper. . . ."
   g) "[T]he top 20 percent of our population own close to 90 percent of the total wealth in this country."

4. Piff explains, "None . . . of the cars in our least expensive category broke the law." Why is this observation about the behavior of people driving inexpensive cars important to Piff's broader argument?

   a) Most Americans drive inexpensive cars.
   b) People driving inexpensive cars can't afford to get a ticket, so they always follow traffic laws.
   c) People driving inexpensive cars are less likely to put their own needs above others and are more likely to follow the rules.
   d) People who feel rich are greedy.

5. Which additional phrase(s) from the text helps you to understand the answer to Question 4? More than one answer may be correct.

   a) "What we found was that as the expensiveness of a car increased, the driver's tendencies to break the law increased as well."
   b) "[W]e looked at whether drivers would stop for a pedestrian. . . ."
   c) "Close to 50 percent of the cars in our most expensive vehicle category broke the law."
   d) "We've even studied cars. . . ."

6. What is Paul Piff's purpose in discussing the different experiments conducted at Berkeley?

   a) He wants to celebrate the accomplishments of the scientists at Berkeley.
   b) He wants to prove that his ideas are real and true.
   c) He wants to show how ideas have been verified by scientific experiments.
   d) He wants to explain what he does in his laboratory at Berkeley.

7. Which question(s) is/are raised but not answered by "Does money make you mean?"

   a) Will achieving the American Dream be possible in the future?
   b) Are there wealthy people who are trying to address economic inequality?
   c) Are rich people poor drivers?
   d) Is the United States more economically unequal than it was in the past?

May be photocopied for classroom use. *Using Informational Text to Teach* The Great Gatsby by Audrey Fisch and Susan Chenelle © 2018 (Lanham, MD: Rowman & Littlefield).

8. Piff writes, "We had a bowl of pretzels positioned off to the side. . . . That allowed us to watch participants' consummatory behavior." By consummatory behavior, Piff means

   a) eating
   b) cheating
   c) meanness
   d) trickiness

9. Why is Piff interested in "participants' consummatory behavior"?

   a) The researchers were studying the rich player's loud behavior.
   b) The researchers were interested in "signs of dominance."
   c) The researchers were interested in other examples of cheating.
   d) The researchers wanted to connect appetite and skill level.

10. In which other paragraph of the transcript is a similar idea about "participants' consummatory behavior" discussed?

    a) "We ran another study where we looked at whether people would be inclined to take candy. . . ."
    b) "We've even studied cars. . . ."
    c) "And beyond the wall of our lab, we're even beginning to see signs of change in society."
    d) "[W]e've been finding in our own laboratory research that small psychological interventions, small nudges in certain directions, can restore levels of egalitarianism. . . ."

WRITING AND DISCUSSION

A. What do the experiments show?

1. **Discuss**: The first experiment under discussion involves a Monopoly game. What are the key issues in this experiment? What conditions did the scientists set up for the game? What observations did the researchers make about the players' behavior during the game? What did the researchers observe about the pretzels? What conclusions do the researchers draw?

2. **Discuss**: After the rigged Monopoly game, Piff describes the ways in which the rich players "talked about why they had inevitably won." He describes an "incredible insight into how the mind makes sense of advantage." What does he mean? How do the rich players' minds make sense of their advantage in the game?

3. **Discuss**: The second experiment under discussion involves people taking candy from a jar. What are the key issues in this experiment? What conclusions do the researchers draw?

4. **Discuss**: The third experiment under discussion involves drivers who do or do not stop for pedestrians. What are the key issues in this experiment? What conclusions do the researchers draw? Represent the data from this experiment in some kind of graph or chart.

5. **Discuss**: The fourth experiment under discussion involves people who watch a brief video about childhood poverty. What are the key issues in this experiment? What conclusions do the researchers draw?

6. **Write**: Paul Piff offers descriptions of several different laboratory experiments in his discussion, "Does money make you mean?" Based on his research, how would you answer his question? How do you feel about the research you have learned about here? What else would you like to know about the research in this area? What experiments would you like to see researchers undertake in relation to this issue? *Use evidence from the reading to explain and explore Piff's experiments.*

B. Does money make Tom mean?

1. **Discuss**: In "Does money make you mean?" Paul Piff writes that the rich players in the rigged Monopoly game were more likely to show "signs of dominance and nonverbal signs, displays of power and celebration." How exactly does Piff indicate that these rich players exhibited their dominance? *Use Table 3.1 to collect and organize your evidence.*

2. **Discuss**: In *Gatsby*, how does rich Tom Buchanan display his dominance, particularly in relation to those less wealthy than he is? *Use Table 3.1 to collect and organize your evidence.*

3. **Write**: Piff writes that his rigged game of Monopoly "can be used as a metaphor for understanding society." Why? What does his rigged Monopoly game reveal about the unfair behavior of those in the game who are unfairly rich? Use Piff's research to analyze Tom's behavior in *Gatsby*. Does money make Tom mean? How does Tom's behavior illustrate the findings of Piff's experiments? *Use evidence from* Gatsby *and the readings to discuss the question of whether money makes Tom mean.*

Table is available for download at http://www.usinginformationaltext.com/student.

C. Is it every man (or woman) for himself (or herself)?

1. **Discuss**: Paul Piff suggests that "the wealthier you are, the more likely you are to pursue a vision of personal success, of achievement and accomplishment, to the detriment of others around you." What does Piff mean by this statement? What does it mean to pursue one's success to the "detriment of others"? How is Piff's theory supported by his research?

2. **Discuss**: Think about how the various characters achieve personal success in *Gatsby*. Are there characters who put their own interests "above the interests and well-being of other people"? How do these characters pursue a vision of success to the detriment of others? Do other characters behave differently? *Use Table 3.2 to collect and organize your responses.*

3. **Write**: In "Does money make you mean?" Paul Piff suggests that, particularly in a climate of economic inequality, the pursuit of success can come at the expense of others. In what ways does *Gatsby* conform to Piff's ideas? Are there characters within the novel who pursue personal success to the detriment of others? Are there characters who do not conform to Piff's ideas? *Use evidence from* Gatsby *and the reading to discuss whether the characters in Fitzgerald's novel support or refute Piff's idea that the wealthy are more likely to put their own self-interest and success above others.*

Table is available for download at http://www.usinginformationaltext.com/student.

CLASS ACTIVITY

Task: Imagine that, instead of sitting around drinking in chapter 2, Tom, Myrtle, Nick, Jordan, Catherine McKee, and Mr. McKee engage in a game of Monopoly. Given what you have learned from Paul Piff, rethink and rewrite a section of this chapter. Use what you have learned about how money makes people such as Tom mean to think about how this game will play out. What will the characters talk about? How will they behave? Which of the characters will cheat and how?

In groups:

1. **Draft your section**: Your new section should include some of the information conveyed in the original chapter 2 but with the scene now transformed into a game of Monopoly. As with Fitzgerald's novel, use Nick to narrate the events in the section.

2. **Perform your section**: Choose your roles and perform your new section of chapter 2. The student who performs the role of Nick should also offer his narrative commentary as part of his performance.

As a class:

3. **Discuss**: Which group best captured both Piff's ideas and key elements of chapter 2 and the characters in *Gatsby*? Why? How do the performances help you reflect on the essential question: Does money make people such as Tom mean?

In groups:

4. **Revise your section**: Based on your performance and class discussion, create a revised version of your new section of chapter 2.

Individually:

5. **Reflect**: Write a reflection in which you explain what your group was trying to accomplish with your new section of chapter 2. Justify (with textual evidence from *Gatsby* and Piff) your choices in your section. Explain as well how your section reflects your understanding of Fitzgerald's text as well as your insights about how the different characters' behaviors might be predicted by Piff's research. Discuss how your group decided to revise your section, based on your performance, the performances of the other groups, and your discussion of all of the performances. Finally, reflect on what you learned from the performance and from the class discussion about the essential question: Does money make people such as Tom mean?

CLASS ACTIVITY RUBRIC

Category	4—Excellent	3—Good	2—Satisfactory	1—Unsatisfactory
New section of chapter 2 (presentation of knowledge and ideas)	Section demonstrates strong and insightful comprehension of the novel and the issues in the informational text	Section demonstrates solid comprehension of the novel and the issues in the informational text	Section demonstrates some comprehension of the novel and the issues in the informational text, though the section may be vague or ineffective	Section does not demonstrate comprehension of the novel and/or the issues in the informational text
Reflection (cite relevant and sufficient textual evidence)	Reflection makes clear, insightful arguments based on substantial specific evidence from the novel and informational text	Reflection makes clear arguments based on specific evidence from the novel and informational text	Reflection makes arguments that may be vague or not clearly based on evidence from the novel and informational text	Reflection does not make arguments based on evidence from the novel and informational text
Vocabulary (use domain-specific vocabulary)	Several "words to own" from the unit are used correctly in the new section and/or reflection	Some "words to own" from the unit are used correctly in the new section and/or reflection	One or more "words to own" from the unit are used in the new section and/or reflection but not correctly or effectively	No "words to own" from the unit are used in the new section and/or reflection
Documentation and style (in-text citation and works cited)	Reflection conforms to the appropriate style guidelines (MLA) for in-text citation and works cited; new section follows appropriate style and format for a novel	Reflection conforms with limited errors to the appropriate style guidelines (MLA) for in-text citation and works cited; new section follows appropriate style and format for a novel with limited errors	Reflection attempts to conform to the appropriate style guidelines (MLA) for in-text citation and works cited but does so ineffectively or inaccurately; new section attempts to follow appropriate style and format for a novel but does so ineffectively or inaccurately	Reflection does not conform to the appropriate style guidelines (MLA) for in-text citation and works cited; new section does not follow appropriate style and format for a novel

May be photocopied for classroom use. *Using Informational Text to Teach* The Great Gatsby by Audrey Fisch and Susan Chenelle © 2018 (Lanham, MD: Rowman & Littlefield).

UNIT 4

Who Is to Blame in the Black Sox Scandal and in *Gatsby*?

TEACHER'S GUIDE

Overview

Even students who are fervent baseball fans may find it difficult to fully appreciate what the sport meant to Americans in the early twentieth century. In 1919, baseball, called America's pastime, was the only sport in the United States to have a professional league. Individually, professional baseball players such as Shoeless Joe Jackson of the White Sox were idolized as both local and national heroes.

As New York radio personality Jean Shepard related on the air in the 1960s, when his father, who had grown up on Chicago's South Side, died, he still considered the Black Sox scandal "the major tragedy of his entire life." Though professional athletes are still looked to as role models, it is no longer presumed that they will act as such on or off the field or uphold the ideals of fair play, good sportsmanship, and generally honorable behavior that are supposed to govern our penchant for competition.

On the other hand, students, especially those who are sports fans, may still be surprised that players would conspire to lose something as big as the World Series, especially for such an arguably small payoff.

In this section, we offer two accounts of the scandal, one contemporary and one written in 2012. The first is an excerpt of a 1920 *New York Times* article on the indictment of the eight players for the White Sox who conspired with gamblers to fix the Series, which includes testimony from one of the primary players involved.

The second piece, from a sports journalism blog, describes how newspapers reported on the scandal at the time, including which parties in the conspiracy were blamed and which were not. Dezenhall focuses, in particular, on how the combination of anti-Semitism and the myth of the American baseball player shaped media coverage of the scandal.

The readings in this unit will help students understand the broader importance of the scandal to American society in order to appreciate the symbolic resonance of the scandal in *Gatsby*.

Timing

These excerpts work best after students have read chapter 4, when the scandal is mentioned during Nick's lunch with Gatsby and Meyer Wolfsheim.

Consider the following guidelines regarding when to undertake the different activities:

Essential Question for Discussion and Writing	Objective	Suggested Timing	Suggested Rubric	Additional Research
A. Who's to blame in the Black Sox scandal? RI 1, 2, 3, 4, 5, 6, 8, 9, 10 W 1, 2, 4, 5, 9, 10 SL 1, 4 L 1, 2, 3, 5, 6	SW analyze a contemporary news report on the Black Sox scandal and a blog post about newspaper coverage of it in order to write an essay identifying bias in the newspaper article and evaluate their effects on the reader.	Any time—this set cf questions doesn't require any knowledge of *Gatsby*.	A	N

Essential Question for Discussion and Writing	Objective	Suggested Timing	Suggested Rubric	Additional Research
B. Who's to blame for Gatsby's crimes? RL 1, 2, 3, 4, 5, 6, 8, 9, 10 RI 1, 2, 3, 4, 5, 6, 8, 9, 10 W 1, 2, 4, 5, 9, 10 SL 1, 4 L 1, 2, 3, 5, 6	SW analyze Nick/Fitzgerald's portrayal of Meyer Wolfsheim in order to write an essay evaluating how anti-Semitism might be used to shift blame away from Gatsby as it was to shift blame away from the players in the Black Sox scandal.	After chapter 4 (when Nick meets Meyer Wolfsheim) and/or after finishing the novel (following Nick's conversation with Wolfsheim after Gatsby's death)	A	N
Class Activities				
Create infographics that illustrate different views of the Black Sox scandal and Gatsby's crimes RL 1, 2, 3, 4, 5, 6, 10 RI 1, 2, 3, 4, 5, 6, 8, 9, 10 W 1, 2, 3, 4, 5, 6, 8, 9, 10 SL 1, 4 L 1, 2, 3, 5, 6	SW use their understanding of the readings and the novel to create infographics that depict opposing views of who is to blame for the Black Sox scandal and/or Gatsby's crimes.	After finishing the novel	Rubric included	N

NOTES ON THE READINGS

- These two pieces from two very different sources offer students an excellent opportunity to think critically about the credibility and point of view of media coverage. Although the contemporary excerpt from the *New York Times* might seem to be more objective and authoritative, the blog excerpt, through careful analysis of varied sources, offers students the opportunity to consider bias in the newspaper article. (Teachers may want to have students look at the complete post, which can be found on the Shirley Povich Center for Sports Journalism website, so that they can see the extensive citations in the original, which we have omitted here.)
- These readings directly relate to a brief moment in *Gatsby*, when Nick meets Meyer Wolfsheim during lunch with Gatsby, but they also can help students understand how the anti-Semitism that was prevalent during the 1920s manifested itself in society. Teachers may want to undertake this unit after studying the readings on white nationalism in unit 2, "What Is Tom Worried About—Is Civilization Going to Pieces?"

SUGGESTED MEDIA LINKS

- The 1988 film *Eight Men Out*, starring John Cusack and directed by John Sayles, dramatizes the scandal, emphasizing how the gamblers preyed upon the conspiring players' bitterness toward their miserly team owner, Charles Comiskey.
- The last half hour of the third episode of Ken Burns's documentary series *Baseball* focuses in detail on how the scandal and coverage of it played out and even dramatizes a small part of Shoeless Joe Jackson's grand jury testimony. The images throughout the episode make clear how different the game was back then, particularly in terms of the meager equipment and uniforms the players had. In addition, about half way through the episode, before the segment on the scandal, poet Donald Hall talks about how baseball was a vital avenue for assimilation into American society for immigrant boys and men.
- An excerpt of AMC's docudrama series *Making of the Mob: New York* features a brief profile of Arnold Rothstein, the model for Meyer Wolfsheim. A longer segment on the Bloodletters and Badmen YouTube channel details Rothstein's career and influence, including a brief but engaging description of his involvement in the Black Sox scandal and how he handled being called to testify during the players' trial.

- A section on the Famous Trials website, maintained by University of Missouri-Kansas City law professor Douglas O. Lindner, features links to numerous primary documents related to the scandal as well as a trove of photos, including a very intriguing one of the players and jurors after the verdict.
- In a 1960s broadcast, New York radio personality Jean Shepard describes the impact the scandal had on young, working-class boys such as his father who grew up on the south side of Chicago in the shadow of Comiskey Park, "the only thing to have any majesty, any grandeur, any drama in their whole life." The broadcast has been incorporated into a YouTube video posted by danieljbmitchell, along with photos from the period. Though the sound quality is marred by static, and Shepard digresses at times, some fantastic bits capture the stature baseball and its players had at the time and what an enormous betrayal the scandal was to baseball fans—particularly because, as Shepard explains, the players of that time "were like the guys who came to see them; they were all poor working men." Indeed, Shepard goes on to explain how poorly even star players such as Shoeless Joe Jackson were paid.

VOCABULARY WARM-UP

> **WORDS TO OWN:** adhere, collusion, complicity, conspiracy, culprit, debauchery, degenerate, disparage, fix, incriminatory, indict, palatable, pervade, throw, unscrupulous, vilify

Section A: Use context clues: Read the following sentences and use context clues to determine the meaning of the italicized words.

1. When students see a classmate being bullied, they sometimes look the other way. However, I am determined to always stand up against bullying because not saying anything is an act of *complicity* with the bullies. I would be helping them rather than the person being bullied. Why might someone decide to be *complicit* with a bully?

2. There were rumors of a *conspiracy* to rig or fix the outcome of the vote for this year's prom king and queen. Many suspected that the president of the student council had *conspired* with her friends on the student council to make sure that she and her boyfriend won. What does it mean to *conspire* about something? Does a *conspiracy* involve doing something good or bad, alone or with other people?

3. Today, many families observe religious or cultural holidays in new ways, whereas others strictly *adhere* to traditional ways of celebrating them, always serving the same foods or carrying out the same customs or rituals. What does it mean to *adhere* to something in this context? Does your family change things for certain holidays, or do you *adhere* to the way you have always done things? Do you think it's important to *adhere* to tradition when celebrating holidays? Why or why not?

4. The girl was upset because someone told her that one of her close friends had made *disparaging* comments about her behind her back. She was tempted to start spreading the same kind of negative rumors about her friend to get back at her, but she decided the drama wasn't worth it. How would you feel if someone was making *disparaging* comments about you?

5. Despite what had seemed like a mountain of *incriminatory* evidence, the defendant was found not guilty of all charges. The jury thought the defense attorney had successfully discredited the evidence that made her client seem guilty, so they acquitted the defendant. If you were a juror in a trial, what kinds of evidence would seem most *incriminating* to you?

6. Federal aviation authorities were determined to find the *culprit* for the plane crash. The pilot who survived said a bird strike knocked out the engines, while airline executives blamed the pilot. How do you think the investigators would go about determining the true *culprit*?

Section B: More context clues: Here your task is to use context clues to understand the italicized word's meaning AND to practice your context clues skills.

1. The *New York Times* reported, "Seven star players of the Chicago White Sox and one former player were *indicted*, charged with complicity in a conspiracy with gamblers to 'fix' the 1919 World Series." What does it mean to be *indicted*?

    a) convicted of a crime
    b) accused of a crime
    c) found innocent of a crime
    d) called to testify as a witness in a trial

2. Which word(s) from the sentence in Question 1 best helps the reader understand the meaning of *indicted*?

    a) gamblers
    b) evidence
    c) charged
    d) World Series

3. According to Stuart Dezenhall, the rumored involvement of gangster Arnold Rothstein, whose Jewish identity suggested he was somehow dishonest to many Americans, "provid[ed] a character for reporters to *vilify* rather than attacking the cheating players." What does it mean to *vilify* someone?

    a) validate
    b) praise
    c) defend
    d) condemn

4. Which word(s) from the sentence in Question 3 best helps you understand the meaning of *vilify*?

    a) rumored
    b) Jewish gangster
    c) attacking
    d) reporters

5. According to Stuart Dezenhall, reporters quoted the grand jury foreman of the Black Sox trial as saying that gamblers were "corrupting players." Robert Edgren of the *New York Evening World* hoped the government would "run down those responsible for the *debauchery* of baseball players. . . ." What does *debauchery* mean here?

    a) innocence
    b) immoral behavior
    c) celebrity
    d) testimony

6. Which word(s) from the sentences in Question 5 best help you understand the meaning of *debauchery*?

    a) bleeding baseball
    b) run down
    c) responsible
    d) corrupting

Section C: Sometimes common words are used in uncommon ways. **Use the dictionary** in order to understand the uncommon meanings of the italicized common words.

1. The *New York Times* reported that eight current and former players for the Chicago White Sox were "charged with complicity in a conspiracy with gamblers to 'fix' the 1919 World Series." Obviously, the players did not repair something broken. How is *fix* being used here? What did the players do?

2. After being charged, two of the participants confessed that they had deliberately *thrown* the championship to Cincinnati. Did the Chicago players literally throw something to the Cincinnati players? How is *thrown* being used here?

3. According to Stuart Dezenhall, journalists "attempted to protect baseball's reputation" and blame the scandal on a culprit from outside the world of baseball who was more *palatable* to Americans. Dezenhall, of course, doesn't mean that the culprit tasted better. What does *palatable* mean in this case?

4. Dezenhall argues that "newspaper coverage of the scandal *adhered* to the cultural norms of the late Progressive Era." Clearly, newspaper coverage can't physically stick to something. How is the word *adhered* being used here? What does it mean for newspaper coverage to *adhere* to the ideas and ways of thinking in the Progressive Era?

Section D: Use the dictionary to look up the italicized words and answer the following questions based on their definitions.

1. According to Stuart Dezenhall, "shock *pervaded* the baseball world when Cincinnati won four of the first five games" of the 1919 World Series. What does it mean if "shock *pervaded* the baseball world"? Were few or most baseball fans shocked?

2. Sometimes powerful leaders or politicians are accused of being *unscrupulous* in the way they accomplish their goals. Is *unscrupulous* behavior ever justified in order to achieve a worthy accomplishment? Would you support a leader who was *unscrupulous*? Why or why not?

3. Throughout history there have been backlashes against what some see as *degenerate* behavior. However, what is considered *degenerate* behavior in one time can be considered acceptable in another time. Why do you think attitudes about certain so-called *degenerate* behaviors change in this way?

4. Some countries have very high crime rates due to *collusion* between the police and drug traffickers. What would this mean? Why do you think a police officer would *collude* with drug dealers?

5. If you were a lawyer, what do you think you would do first if your client was *indicted*? Is an *indictment* an indication of guilt?

6. Some university honor codes consider it to be a violation not just to cheat, but also to be *complicit* in an act of cheating. For example, if you let someone copy your homework, you might be considered just as guilty of cheating as if you copied another's homework. Or if you saw someone cheating and didn't speak up, you might be considered *complicit* in the act of cheating. What do you think is the difference between cheating and being *complicit* in an act of cheating? Why do you think a university might consider both a violation of the honor code?

Section E: Practice using the word correctly by choosing the correct form of the word(s) that best fits in the blank within the following sentences.

1. The boy realized that his downfall came from being _____ in choosing his friends; he didn't think carefully enough about whether they were good or bad influences on him.

   a) unscrupulously
   b) unscrupulous
   c) unscrupulousness
   d) unscrupulosity

2. The young woman had few friends because she always spoke so _____ about people; she was not a kind or generous person.

   a) disparage
   b) disparaging
   c) disparagingly
   d) disparaged

3. Chinese restaurant owners in the United States often change how they make traditional Chinese dishes in order to make them more _____ to American tastes.

   a) palatably
   b) palatableness
   c) palatable
   d) palatability

4. Many suspected that the security analyst had been _____ with the enemy; he was soon indicted for sharing classified materials with terrorists.

   a) collusion
   b) colluding
   c) collude
   d) colluded

5. To those who follow a strict religious code of conduct, the behavior of American society may seem _____.

   a) degenerate
   b) degenerating
   c) degeneratingly
   d) degenerately

6. In the late 1950s, TV viewers were outraged to find out that their favorite game shows were sometimes _____ so that a popular contestant would win no matter how skilled he or she was at the game.

   a) fix
   b) fixed
   c) fixing
   d) fixated

May be photocopied for classroom use. *Using Informational Text to Teach* The Great Gatsby by Audrey Fisch and Susan Chenelle © 2018 (Lanham, MD: Rowman & Littlefield).

Section F: Vocabulary skits
Use the model sentences and definitions to understand the words in question. Create a skit in which you address the given topic. Every member of the group must use the vocabulary word at least once during your performance of the skit.

1. *incriminatory*—implying someone's guilt of a crime or error
   - The lawyer argued that the evidence against her client was merely circumstantial and not *incriminatory*.
   - The gangster was determined to find out who had *incriminated* him to the police.
   - You should always be careful about posting photos of yourself online; you never know what could be considered *incriminatory* to a potential employer.

Scenario: Create a skit in which a teacher is trying to determine who among a group of students is responsible for leading the widespread cheating on a recent test. What evidence might *incriminate* a particular student? What might each student say in order to avoid *incriminating* himself or herself?

2. *complicit*—being involved with others in an illegal or questionable act
   - Some accused the media of being *complicit* in causing the war because it did not do enough to question the government's arguments in favor of invasion.
   - The study that claimed to have found cigarettes to be healthy was quickly discredited because the scientists who produced it were *complicit* with the tobacco industry.
   - If one group of people is born with certain advantages over other groups of people, does that make the privileged people *complicit* in discrimination?

Scenario: Schools today often spend a lot of time trying to address or prevent bullying. Create a skit in which a group of students discusses the causes and effects of bullying and how best to address or prevent it. Is bullying just the fault of the bully, or are those who stand by also *complicit*, whether or not they join in?

3. *disparage*—to discredit or speak ill of someone or something

- In some countries, it is illegal to make *disparaging* remarks about the government.
- Saying *disparaging* things about someone often backfires; it can make the speaker look worse than the person he or she was trying to *disparage*.
- Though the presidential campaign tried to *disparage* the opponent, voters ignored the accusations and continued to support the campaign's rival.

Scenario: Create a skit in which a group of students are discussing how to get the school administration to reinstate students' privilege to leave campus for lunch. Some students in the group have been making *disparaging* comments about the policy and the administration on social media since the new policy went into effect. Other students in the group are concerned that *disparaging* the administration isn't helping their cause.

4. *culprit*—the person or party responsible for a crime or misdeed

- The girl had accused her little brother of destroying her shoes, but it turned out that their dog was the *culprit*.
- The scientists were trying frantically to find the *culprit* for an illness that was rapidly spreading throughout the country; some thought the *culprit* was bacterial, whereas others suspected it was a virus.
- Though the bank robber initially got away, the police soon caught up with and arrested the *culprit*.

Scenario: The school administration has asked the student council to help identify the *culprit* behind a recent series of vandalism incidents in the school. Create a skit in which the members of the student council discuss strategies for finding the *culprit*.

May be photocopied for classroom use. *Using Informational Text to Teach* The Great Gatsby by Audrey Fisch and Susan Chenelle © 2018 (Lanham, MD: Rowman & Littlefield).

ESSENTIAL QUESTION: WHO IS TO BLAME IN THE BLACK SOX SCANDAL AND IN *GATSBY*?

Introduction to the Unit

Today, sports fans have, unfortunately, become accustomed to scandals involving professional athletes, both in their personal lives as well as in their professional careers. For example, nearly every professional sport—from baseball to cycling—has been touched by some kind of performance-enhancing drug scandal. However, when eight players for the Chicago White Sox were charged with deliberately losing the 1919 World Series in exchange for money, the nation was deeply shocked, particularly given the importance of baseball, often called America's pastime, as the ultimate symbol of American culture. In chapter 4, Nick meets Meyer Wolfsheim, who is identified as "the man who fixed the World's Series back in 1919." Wolfsheim is a fictionalized version of Arnold Rothstein, a Jewish gangster often held responsible for the so-called Black Sox scandal.

The two pieces in this unit help us understand the Black Sox scandal and why it had such a deep effect on the American public. The first is an excerpt from a *New York Times* report on the indictment of the eight baseball players who conspired with gamblers to "fix" the series, including testimony from one of the primary players involved. The second piece is from a blog on sports journalism that describes how newspapers reported on the shocking revelations at the time, including who was and was not blamed.

> **Reflect on the essential question:** Why do you think "fixing" the World Series would have been such a big deal in 1919? Would people today be surprised and upset by a cheating scandal in professional sports? Can you think of recent equivalent sports scandals? How have people reacted to these scandals?
>
> **Reflect on the introduction:** Why do you think baseball is often considered "the ultimate symbol of American culture"? What qualities about America might baseball represent?

May be photocopied for classroom use. *Using Informational Text to Teach* The Great Gatsby by Audrey Fisch and Susan Chenelle © 2018 (Lanham, MD: Rowman & Littlefield).

READING #1: EXCERPT FROM A NEWS STORY ON THE "BLACK SOX" SCANDAL

Introduction

Below is an excerpt of a news story published in the *New York Times* about the indictment of eight baseball players involved in what came to be known as the "Black Sox" scandal. All eight players ultimately were acquitted of all criminal charges due to legal technicalities and lost evidence but were permanently banned from playing major league baseball.

Left fielder "Shoeless" Joe Jackson, who still has the third highest lifetime batting average in major league baseball history, has never been inducted into the Baseball Hall of Fame because of his involvement in the conspiracy. This piece features the testimony of one of the key players, star pitcher Eddie Cicotte, who explains how the "fix" came about and why he participated.

> **Reflect on the introduction:** The introduction indicates that all the players were acquitted of criminal charges yet they were still permanently banned from baseball. What does this outcome suggest to you about the scandal?
>
> **Reflect** on the kind of piece you will be reading and where it was published. How reliable do you think the information presented here will be? Why?

From "Eight White Sox Players Are Indicted on Charge of Fixing 1919 World Series; Cicotte Got $10,000 and Jackson $5,000"

Published in the *New York Times*, September 29, 1920

Chicago, Sept. 28—Seven star players of the Chicago White Sox and one former player were *indicted* late this afternoon, charged with *complicity* in a *conspiracy* with gamblers to "*fix*" the 1919 World Series. The *indictments* were based on evidence obtained for the Cook County Grand Jury by Charles A. Comiskey, owner of the White Sox, and after confessions by two of the players told how the world's championship was *thrown* to

> **Reflect on the title:** What information is included in this headline and how does the information shape the tone of the headline and the article? Given the subtitle of the headline, what perspective do you think the article offers about the guilt of the players?
>
> **Vocabulary:** The news article reports that eight players "were indicted . . . charged with complicity in a conspiracy with gamblers to 'fix' the 1919 World Series." What have the players been accused of doing? Have they been proven guilty? State this idea in your own words.

Cincinnati and how they had received money or were "double-crossed" by the gamblers.

The eight players *indicted* are: Eddie Cicotte, star pitcher; "Shoeless Joe" Jackson, left fielder and heavy hitter; Oscar "Hap" Felsch, center fielder; Charles "Swede" Risberg, short-stop; George "Buck" Weaver, third baseman; Arnold Gandil, former first baseman; Claude Williams, pitcher; Fred McMullin, utility player.

The specific charge against the eight players is "*conspiracy* to commit an illegal act," which is punishable by five years' imprisonment or a fine up to $10,000 . . .

No sooner had the news of the *indictments* become public than Comiskey suspended the seven players, wrecking the team he had given years to build up and almost certainly forfeiting his chances to beat out Cleveland for the American League pennant. . . .

Cicotte admitt[ed] receiving $10,000 and *throwing* two games, and Jackson admitt[ed] receiving $5,000 of $20,000 promised him by the gamblers and [told] of his efforts to defeat his own team.

CICOTTE BREAKS DOWN AND WEEPS

"My God! think of my children," he cried. Cicotte has two small children.

"I never did anything I regretted so much in my life," he continued. "I would give anything in the world if I could undo my acts in the last world's series. I've played a crooked game and I have lost, and I am here to tell the whole truth."

> **Vocabulary:** What does it mean that the "world's championship was thrown to Cincinnati"? What does the players' claim that they were "'double-crossed' by the gamblers" mean? State these ideas in your own words.
>
> **Notice** that the article indicates that eight players were involved in the scandal. Why would it take so many players to successfully throw a World Series?
>
> **Notice:** How did the owner of the White Sox respond to the indictments of the players? What do you think of his actions? Why do you think the news article notes that his response resulted in "wrecking the team he had given years to build up and almost certainly forfeiting his chances to beat out Cleveland for the American League pennant"?
>
> **Notice** the subheading here. Why do you think it is included? What does it add to the article for the reader?

"I've lived a thousand years in the last year."

Describing how two games were *thrown* to Cincinnati, Cicotte, according to court officials, said:

"In the first game at Cincinnati . . . I wasn't putting a thing on the ball. You could have read the trade mark on it when I lobbed the ball up to the plate."

"In the fourth game, played at Chicago, which I also lost, I deliberately intercepted a throw from the outfield to the plate which might have cut off a run. I muffed the ball on purpose."

"At another time in the same game I purposely made a wild throw. All the runs scored against me were due to my own deliberate errors. I did not try to win."

Cicotte . . . confessed first to Comiskey. He went to the latter's office early in the morning.

"I don't know what you'll think of me," he said, "but I got to tell you how I double-crossed you. Mr. Comiskey, I did double-cross you. I'm a crook, and I got $10,000 for being a crook."

> **Notice:** Cicotte says that he's "lived a thousand years in the last year." What does he mean by this? How does this statement contribute to his testimony?
>
> **Key idea:** What does Cicotte mean when he says he "wasn't putting a thing on the ball. You could have read the trade mark on it when I lobbed the ball up to the plate"? What did he do to help "throw" the first game to Cincinnati? What did he do in the later games? State these actions in your own words.
>
> **Notice:** Cicotte first confessed to White Sox owner Charles Comiskey. How would you describe the way Comiskey responds to him, according to the article?

"Don't tell it to me," replied Comiskey, "tell it to the Judge."

Cicotte told it to the Judge in tears and shame, slowly, haltingly, hanging his head, now and then pausing to wipe his streaming eyes.

"Risberg and Gandil and McMullin were at me for a week before the world's series started," he said. "They wanted me to go crooked. I didn't know—I needed the money.

I had the wife and the kids. The wife and kids don't know this. I don't know what they'll think."

SAYS HE NEEDED IT TO PAY MORTGAGE

"I bought a farm. There was a $4,000 mortgage on it. There isn't any mortgage on it now. I paid it off with the crooked money."

"The eight of us [the eight under *indictment*] got together in my room three or four days before the games started. Gandil was the master of ceremonies. We talked about *throwing* the series. Decided we could get away with it. We agreed to do it."

"I was thinking of the wife and kids and how I needed the money. I told them I had to have the cash in advance. . . . I wanted it before I pitched a ball."

"We all talked quite a while about it, I and the seven others. Yes, all of us decided to do our best to *throw* the games to Cincinnati." . . .

"The day before I went to Cincinnati I put it up to them squarely for the last time, that there would be nothing doing unless I had the money."

"That night I found the money under my pillow. There was $10,000. I counted it. I don't know who put it there, but it was there. It was my price. I had sold out 'Commy'; I had sold out the other boys: sold them for $10,000 to pay off a mortgage on a farm, and for the wife and kids.

> **Notice:** According to Cicotte, how did he become involved in the conspiracy? Who are Risberg, Gandil, and McMullin? What is Cicotte suggesting when he says they "were at me for a week before the world's series started"?

> **Notice:** According to the testimony and the subheading here, why did Cicotte become involved in the conspiracy? Does it seem odd that a star professional athlete was worried about being able to pay his mortgage? What does this suggest about how professional athletes were paid back then, compared to now?

> **Notice:** Cicotte says that the eight players gathered in his hotel room but describes Gandil as "the master of ceremonies." What does this mean? How does this fit with the way Cicotte is presenting his own participation in the conspiracy?

"If I had reasoned what that meant to me, the taking of that dirty crooked money—the hours of mental torture, the days and nights of living with an unclean mind; the weeks and months of going along with six of the seven crooked players and holding a guilty secret, and of going along with the boys who had stayed straight and clean and honest boys who had nothing to trouble them—say, it was hell."

> **Key idea:** Based on the end of his testimony, how does Cicotte feel now about his involvement in fixing the World Series? What do you think he is trying to convince the Grand Jury of with this statement?

"Eight White Sox Players Are Indicted on Charge of Fixing 1919 World Series; Cicotte Got $10,000 and Jackson $5,000." *New York Times,* September 29, 1920.

READING #2: EXCERPT FROM A BLOG POST PUBLISHED ON A WEBSITE ABOUT SPORTS JOURNALISM

Introduction

Below is an excerpt from an essay by Stuart Dezenhall, who wrote several papers on sports history when he was a graduate student and went on to work in public relations for multiple professional sports teams. The essay, published on the Shirley Povich Center for Sports Journalism website, describes how newspaper coverage of the "Black Sox" scandal reflected the social and cultural context of the late Progressive Era in America, which "put a premium on the purity of Americans' pastime [baseball] and the expulsion of corruption," particularly in terms of whom journalists were ready to blame and whom they were willing to give the benefit of the doubt.

From "Newspaper Coverage of the 1919 Black Sox Scandal" by Stuart Dezenhall

In October 1919, sportswriters, fans and bookies expected the Chicago White Sox to easily defeat the Cincinnati Reds in the World Series. With betting lines favoring Chicago to win in the best-of-nine series, shock *pervaded* the baseball world when Cincinnati won four of the first five games. The White Sox won the next two games, restoring a sense of normalcy and cutting the Reds' lead in the series to 4-3. On October 9, with a 10-5 victory in Chicago, the Cincinnati Reds claimed the title.

The surprising result of the 1919 World Series led to baseball's infamous "Black Sox" scandal, which culminated in the banishment of eight White Sox players who

---

> **Reflect on the introduction:** What do you learn from the introduction about the author of this piece and the place of publication for this article? How reliable do you think the information presented here will be? Why?
>
> **Notice** the reference to the "late Progressive Era." What kinds of things were people trying to do during the Progressive Era? What issues were they concerned about? (Check Wikipedia, if necessary.)
>
> **Vocabulary:** What is a bookie? (Use the dictionary, if necessary.) How might a bookie be involved in setting expectations about who will win a sports competition? What does it mean that "betting lines favor[ed] Chicago to win"? State this idea in your own words.
>
> **Vocabulary:** According to the essay, the "Black Sox" scandal "culminated in the banishment of eight White Sox players." What does this mean? What were the players "banished" from?

May be photocopied for classroom use. *Using Informational Text to Teach* The Great Gatsby by Audrey Fisch and Susan Chenelle © 2018 (Lanham, MD: Rowman & Littlefield).

had accepted money to *throw* games, netting *conspiring* gamblers millions. The newspaper coverage of the scandal *adhered* to the cultural norms of the late Progressive Era to appeal to a public that put a premium on the purity of Americans' pastime and the expulsion of corruption. The reporting focused on keeping the brand of baseball as clean as possible—dismissing early, unfounded rumors of foul play and eventually highlighting the role of outside influence in the corruption, primarily that of Jewish gangsters.

Baseball was linked to nationalism;—it was patriotic and protected from outside corruption. With the national mindset obsessed with un-American corruption and their own circulation to consider, newspapers sought to preserve the image of baseball and covered the scandal accordingly.

Anti-Semitism was a pillar of the Americanization movement during the Progressive Era, which featured waves of Jewish immigration from Europe. Jews made quick progress in America and were among the most successful immigrant groups, both culturally and financially, and were thus deemed a "dangerous force undermining the nation."

At first, before any proof of wrongdoing was available, journalists protected the White Sox, attributing the rumors of foul play to one uninformed reporter or sore-losing gamblers. An outside influence in the form of Jewish gangster Arnold Rothstein entered the rumor mill, providing a character for reporters to *vilify* rather than attacking the cheating players.

The first stories of *conspiracy* were written by Hugh Fullerton of the Chicago Herald and Examiner. Fullerton questioned the integrity of some White Sox players, counting seven suspicious plays. Fullerton only vaguely suggested that some players

> **Notice:** According to the article, gamblers "nett[ed] millions" from the scandal. How does that compare to what the conspiring players were paid?
>
> **Key idea:** Dezenhall claims that "newspaper coverage of the scandal adhered to the cultural norms of the late Progressive Era." What does it mean to "adhere to cultural norms"?
>
> **Key idea:** How did Americans feel about baseball at the time? How did this affect newspaper coverage of the scandal, according to Dezenhall?
>
> **Key idea:** Anti-Semitism refers to hatred toward or bias against Jewish people. What does the information here suggest about why anti-Semitism was prevalent during the Progressive Era? Why were Jews considered by some to be "a dangerous force undermining the nation"?

May be photocopied for classroom use. *Using Informational Text to Teach* The Great Gatsby by Audrey Fisch and Susan Chenelle © 2018 (Lanham, MD: Rowman & Littlefield). Excerpts from "Newspaper Coverage of the 1919 Black Sox Scandal" by Stuart Dezenhall. Reprinted by permission of the author. All rights reserved.

might not have given full effort . . . implying that a suspect few spoiled the team's success for others.

Papers that wrote about the Series after its conclusion *disparaged* the play of the losing team but generally did not believe foul play was a factor, concluding that a *fixed* series was unrealistically *conspiratorial*. . . .

Lingering rumors led to the MLB's official investigation nearly a full year after the World Series ended. Even with seemingly *incriminatory* evidence, newspapers nevertheless focused on the corruption of the game by gangsters, not players. Reporters quoted the grand jury foreman saying, "Chicago, New York, Cincinnati and St. Louis gamblers were bleeding baseball and corrupting players." Robert Edgren of the *New York Evening World* hoped the government would "run down those responsible for the *debauchery* of baseball players," and explained that the players, "little more than grownup boys," were "victims of shrewd, smooth, entirely *unscrupulous* gamblers."

As more names appeared in testimony, a clearer picture was forming that gave journalists more ammunition to focus on the dark forces preying on players, including . . . Arnold Rothstein. It was far more culturally acceptable to discuss the greed and immorality of a Jewish outlaw than it was to heap blame on national heroes. . . . As the *Sporting News* wrote, "There are no lengths to which the crop of lean-faced and long-nosed gamblers of these *degenerate* days will go," referencing the easily vilified Jewish gangster.

> **Notice:** Who was given the benefit of the doubt in early reporting on the rumors about possible wrongdoing in the 1919 World Series? Who was quickly blamed despite the absence of any proof? Why do you think this was the case?
>
> **Key idea:** How did sports reporters first explain the surprising loss of the World Series by the White Sox? Why do you think they were inclined to "conclud[e] that a fixed series was unrealistically conspiratorial"?
>
> **Key idea:** When evidence of a "fix" began to emerge, whom did reporters then blame? Why? Does their reporting seem fair?
>
> **Vocabulary:** According to the article, the foreman of the grand jury said, "gamblers were bleeding baseball and corrupting players." What does this mean? How is "bleed" being used here? (Use a dictionary, if necessary.) What effect is this "bleeding" having on baseball?

May be photocopied for classroom use. *Using Informational Text to Teach* The Great Gatsby by Audrey Fisch and Susan Chenelle © 2018 (Lanham, MD: Rowman & Littlefield). Excerpts from "Newspaper Coverage of the 1919 Black Sox Scandal" by Stuart Dezenhall. Reprinted by permission of the author. All rights reserved.

On September 28, 1920, a "mystery witness" admitted to the *collusion* and Cicotte, Gandil, Williams, Felsch, Buck Weaver, Fred McMullin, Swede Risberg and star "Shoeless" Joe Jackson were *indicted* for *conspiracy* to commit an illegal act. After protecting the players so fervently prior to the *indictment*, journalists reported the news as "disillusioned fans" and newspapers printed headlines reserved for an outbreak of war or a political assassination. Despite an eventual not-guilty verdict due to legal technicalities and misplaced evidence, [Major League Baseball] promptly banned the eight players for life, an action that appealed to America's Progressive Era penchant for reform.

Journalists rallied behind the banishment that removed a few bad seeds in an otherwise pure sport. . . .

Journalists called the ballplayers cheats only after they admitted to taking money to *throw* games and were banished from the sport but reported on the influence of Jewish gangsters without any such evidence. . . . [T]hey were also significantly influenced by mainstream America's accepted cultural attitudes and love of baseball, and therefore attempted to protect baseball's reputation . . . from external corruptors who were a preferable and *palatable culprit* in baseball's great *fix*.

Dezenhall, Stuart. "Newspaper Coverage of the 1919 Black Sox Scandal." *The Shirley Povich Center for Sports Journalism*, Philip Merrill College of Journalism, 2012, http://povichcenter.org/newspaper-coverage-of-the-1919-black-sox-scandal/.

Key idea: How did reporters respond when the eight players were indicted? What point is Dezenhall making about how the press reported on the illegal behavior of Rothstein and Jewish gangsters as opposed to how they reported on the illegal acts of the baseball players? How does he explain the difference?

Notice: According to the essay, Major League Baseball "promptly banned the eight players for life, an action that appealed to America's Progressive Era penchant for reform." How does this decision align with the values of the Progressive Era? How does removing a "few bad seeds" allow baseball to remain an "otherwise pure sport"?

Vocabulary: Dezenhall closes with the conclusion that journalists were attempting to protect baseball "from external corruptors who were a preferable and palatable culprit in baseball great fix." Put this into your own words. Who were the external corruptors? Why were they a preferable and palatable culprit?

Reflect on Dezenhall's conclusion. What is his point about how journalists reported on this story? Do you think social and cultural values and biases could affect reporting on sports or other issues today?

CHECK FOR UNDERSTANDING

1. What kind of text is "Eight White Sox Players Are Indicted on Charge of Fixing 1919 World Series; Cicotte Got $10,000 and Jackson $5,000"?

    a) news article
    b) editorial
    c) fake news
    d) biography of Eddie Cicotte

2. What is the central idea of Dezenhall's essay?

    a) The eight players accused of throwing the 1919 World Series were innocent.
    b) Newspapers were wrong to blame only the players for the Black Sox scandal.
    c) Newspapers were more willing to blame Jewish gangsters for the scandal than the revered baseball players.
    d) The fixing of the 1919 World Series is the biggest scandal in the history of sports.

3. Which THREE sentences from the text best support the answer to the question above?

    a) "The White Sox won the next two games, restoring a sense of normalcy and cutting the Reds' lead in the series to 4-3."
    b) "The reporting focused on keeping the brand of baseball as clean as possible—dismissing early, unfounded rumors of foul play and eventually highlighting the role of outside influence in the corruption, primarily that of Jewish gangsters."
    c) "Anti-Semitism was a pillar of the Americanization movement during the Progressive Era, which featured waves of Jewish immigration from Europe."
    d) "An outside influence in the form of Jewish gangster Arnold Rothstein entered the rumor mill, providing a character for reporters to vilify rather than attacking the cheating players."
    e) "Fullerton questioned the integrity of some White Sox players, counting seven suspicious plays."
    f) "It was far more culturally acceptable to discuss the greed and immorality of a Jewish outlaw than it was to heap blame on national heroes."
    g) "Journalists rallied behind the banishment that removed a few bad seeds in an otherwise pure sport."

May be photocopied for classroom use. *Using Informational Text to Teach* The Great Gatsby by Audrey Fisch and Susan Chenelle © 2018 (Lanham, MD: Rowman & Littlefield). Excerpts from "Newspaper Coverage of the 1919 Black Sox Scandal" by Stuart Dezenhall. Reprinted by permission of the author. All rights reserved.

4. Dezenhall argues, "With the national mindset obsessed with un-American corruption and their own circulation to consider, newspapers sought to preserve the image of baseball and covered the scandal accordingly." Which paraphrase best explains the author's claim here?

   a) Newspaper coverage, driven by consideration of sales, focused on the innocence of the greatly admired baseball players and blamed influences from outside the sport.
   b) Newspaper coverage of the scandal immediately blamed the players and led the charge in calling for their banishment from baseball.
   c) Newspaper coverage of the scandal downplayed its significance.
   d) Newspaper coverage of the scandal tried to persuade readers to boycott baseball.

5. Which additional phrase(s) from the text helps you to understand the answer to Question 4? More than one answer may be correct.

   a) "Jews made quick progress in America and were among the most successful immigrant groups"
   b) "At first, before any proof of wrongdoing was available, journalists protected the White Sox, attributing the rumors of foul play to one uninformed reporter or sore-losing gamblers"
   c) "Lingering rumors led to the MLB's official investigation nearly a full year after the World Series ended"
   d) "Journalists called the ballplayers cheats only after they admitted to taking money to throw games and were banished from the sport but reported on the influence of Jewish gangsters without any such evidence"

6. What growing sentiment of the time was a key part of the newspapers' bias against Arnold Rothstein?

   a) anti-Americanism
   b) pacifism
   c) teetotalism
   d) anti-Semitism

7. Which question is unanswered by either reading?

    a) Why did the players throw the 1919 World Series?
    b) How did Eddie Cicotte feel about his participation in fixing the 1919 World Series?
    c) Why did newspapers tend to be biased against Jewish gangsters such as Arnold Rothstein?
    d) Why was baseball associated with nationalism, patriotism, and purity?

8. According to the *New York Times* article, "No sooner had the news of the indictments become public than Comiskey suspended the seven players, wrecking the team he had given years to build up and almost certainly *forfeiting* his chances to beat out Cleveland for the American League pennant." What does *forfeiting* mean here?

    a) ensuring
    b) delaying
    c) giving up
    d) publicizing

9. Which word(s) from the sentence above helps you determine the meaning of *forfeiting*?

    a) "No sooner had the news"
    b) "become public"
    c) "wrecking the team"
    d) "beat out Cleveland"

10. What is the purpose of the following sentence in Dezenhall's essay: "Baseball was linked to nationalism;—it was patriotic and protected from outside corruption"?

    a) to explain why baseball was so important to the American public
    b) to explain why gamblers targeted the sport
    c) to show how the conspiring players were able to throw the World Series
    d) to condemn the players for betraying their fans

May be photocopied for classroom use. *Using Informational Text to Teach* The Great Gatsby by Audrey Fisch and Susan Chenelle © 2018 (Lanham, MD: Rowman & Littlefield).

WRITING AND DISCUSSION
A. Who's to blame in the Black Sox scandal?

1. **Discuss**: Analyze Cicotte's testimony as reported by the *New York Times*. How is he depicted in the article? Which parts of the article might make readers sympathize with him? Which parts of the article might make readers despise him? *Use Table 4.1 to collect and organize your evidence.*

2. **Discuss**: According to Dezenhall, "The newspaper coverage of the scandal *adhered* to the cultural norms of the late Progressive Era to appeal to a public that put a premium on the purity of Americans' pastime and the expulsion of corruption. The reporting focused on keeping the brand of baseball as clean as possible—dismissing early, unfounded rumors of foul play and eventually highlighting the role of outside influence in the corruption, primarily that of Jewish gangsters." What evidence and examples does Dezenhall offer for his argument that the newspaper coverage focused on keeping baseball clean and focusing on corrupt outsiders? *Use Table 4.2 to collect and organize your evidence.*

3. **Discuss**: How does the *New York Times* article compare to this description? In what ways does it exemplify Dezenhall's argument? In what ways does it not do so? *Use Tables 4.3 and 4.4 to collect and organize your evidence.*

4. **Write**: Dezenhall notes, "After protecting the players so fervently prior to the *indictment*, journalists reported the news [of the confessions and *indictment*] as 'disillusioned fans.'" The *New York Times* article is a post-*indictment* discussion of the scandal. Do you think it reflects Dezenhall's representation of the media coverage of the Black Sox scandal? How does the article portray Cicotte? After reading the *New York Times* article, whom do you think baseball fans would blame? *Use evidence from both readings to support your response.*

Tables are available for download at http://www.usinginformationaltext.com/student.

B. Who's to blame for Gatsby's crimes?

1. **Discuss**: According to Dezenhall, "Anti-Semitism was a pillar of the Americanization movement during the Progressive Era, which featured waves of Jewish immigration from Europe. Jews made quick progress in America and were among the most successful immigrant groups, both culturally and financially, and were thus deemed a 'dangerous force undermining the nation.'" What evidence does Dezenhall offer to substantiate his claim that anti-Semitism shaped newspaper coverage of the Black Sox scandal? *Use Table 4.5 to collect and organize your evidence.*

2. **Discuss**: Analyze the description of Meyer Wolfsheim in chapter 4. How does Fitzgerald's portrayal of Wolfsheim compare to the anti-Semitic sentiments Dezenhall describes? *Use Table 4.6 to collect and organize your evidence.*

3. **Discuss**: Analyze Nick's conversation with Wolfsheim in chapter 9, as well as Gatsby and Wolfsheim's interactions in chapter 4. What seems to have been the relationship between Wolfsheim and Gatsby? Who has control in the relationship? *Use Table 4.7 to collect and organize your evidence.*

4. **Write**: Who's to blame for Gatsby's crimes? How does Wolfsheim's relationship with Gatsby compare to that of the Jewish gamblers and the Black Sox players? How does the text exploit anti-Semitism to promote the idea that Gatsby was a relatively innocent pawn in the hands of the Jewish gangster, Wolfsheim? *Use evidence from Dezenhall and* Gatsby *in your response.*

5. **Extra credit**: Does the attempt to shift blame away from Gatsby and onto Wolfsheim reflect Nick's perspective? Does it reflect Fitzgerald's? Discuss how Nick's role as the text's unreliable narrator complicates the answers to #4.

Tables are available for download at http://www.usinginformationaltext.com/student.

CLASS ACTIVITY

The fixing of the 1919 World Series involved several people in a conspiracy. Gatsby himself participated in similar schemes in order to achieve his fortune. In both situations, there are differing perspectives on who is to blame.

1. **Create a set of infographics**: Work in a small group to use Piktochart or another online tool to create a set of two infographics that depict either the Black Sox scandal or Gatsby's crimes.

   Option 1: Using the information from the two readings, create two infographics illustrating the Black Sox scandal. One infographic should portray the gangsters as powerful, whereas the other should portray the baseball players in charge.

   Option 2: Using evidence from the novel, create two infographics illustrating Gatsby's crimes, including his transformation from James Gatz into Jay Gatsby. One infographic should portray Wolfsheim and others as the power behind Gatsby's crimes, whereas the other should depict Gatsby as in charge of his own actions.

2. **Present and discuss**: Present your infographics to the class and lead a discussion of how you represented the relationships between the people involved in the Black Sox scandal or Gatsby's crimes in two different ways.

3. **Reflect**: Write a reflection in which you explain what you were trying to accomplish with your infographics. Justify your choices using textual evidence from both the novel and the readings. Explain how each of your infographics portrays one party or another as responsible for the crimes in question. If you created infographics of the Black Sox scandal, compare your set to those created by classmates who focused on Gatsby in their infographics, and vice versa. Reflect on what you learned about how the presentation of information can shape the perception of events.

CLASS ACTIVITY RUBRIC

Category	4—Excellent	3—Good	2—Satisfactory	1—Unsatisfactory
Infographics (presentation of knowledge and ideas)	Infographics demonstrate strong and insightful comprehension of the novel or the informational texts and represent two opposing views of the chosen subject effectively	Infographics demonstrate solid comprehension of the novel or the informational texts and represent two opposing views of the chosen subject effectively	Infographics demonstrate some comprehension of the novel or the informational texts and unevenly represent two opposing views of the chosen subject	Infographics do not demonstrate comprehension of the novel or the informational texts and may not represent two opposing views of the chosen subject effectively
Presentation and discussion (presentation of knowledge and ideas)	Outstanding participation in group presentation and whole-class discussions, showing an outstanding ability to listen and contribute to collaborative discussions	Good participation in group presentation and whole-class discussions, showing a good ability to listen and contribute to collaborative discussions	Limited or uneven participation in group presentation and whole-class discussions, showing a limited or uneven ability to listen and contribute to collaborative discussions	Insufficient or unsuccessful participation in group presentation and whole-class discussions, showing an insufficient ability to listen and contribute to collaborative discussions

May be photocopied for classroom use. *Using Informational Text to Teach* The Great Gatsby by Audrey Fisch and Susan Chenelle © 2018 (Lanham, MD: Rowman & Littlefield).

Category	4—Excellent	3—Good	2—Satisfactory	1—Unsatisfactory
Reflection (cite relevant and sufficient textual evidence)	Reflection makes clear, insightful arguments based on substantial specific evidence from the novel and informational texts	Reflection makes clear arguments based on specific evidence from the novel and informational texts	Reflection makes arguments that may be vague or not clearly based on evidence from the novel and informational texts	Reflection does not make arguments based on evidence from the novel and informational texts
Vocabulary (use domain-specific vocabulary)	Several "words to own" from the unit are used correctly in your scene and/or reflection	Some "words to own" from the unit are used correctly in your scene and/or reflection	One or more "words to own" from the unit are used in your scene and/or reflection but perhaps not correctly or effectively	No "words to own" from the unit are used in your scene and/or reflection
Documentation and style (in-text citation and works cited)	Reflection conforms to the appropriate style guidelines (MLA) for in-text citation and works cited	Reflection conforms with limited errors to the appropriate style guidelines (MLA) for in-text citation and works cited	Reflection attempts to conform to the appropriate style guidelines (MLA) for in-text citation and works cited but does so ineffectively or inaccurately	Reflection does not conform to the appropriate style guidelines (MLA) for in-text citation and works cited

May be photocopied for classroom use. *Using Informational Text to Teach* The Great Gatsby by Audrey Fisch and Susan Chenelle © 2018 (Lanham, MD: Rowman & Littlefield).

UNIT 5

Everyone Is Drinking, So Why Does Prohibition Matter in *Gatsby*?

TEACHER'S GUIDE

Overview

Prohibition is central to students' understanding of the privileged world of *Gatsby*, in which the rules of the ordinary world don't apply to those with power and money. The readings in this section allow students to understand some of the basic legal elements of Prohibition—including the ways in which the Eighteenth Amendment was distinctly vague on what exactly was prohibited, and the National Prohibition Act (also known as the Volstead Act) created a complicated set of exemptions from Prohibition and a blueprint for corruption.

We also include a newspaper piece from the *New York Times* that, in a jaunty and ironic tone, illustrates the specific climate of noncompliance with Prohibition in New York City and documents the well-known association of drugstores with bootlegging. With this unit, students can begin to think through how alcohol consumption and bootlegging allow Fitzgerald to explore and critique the insular and corrupt world of *Gatsby*.

Timing

The readings in this unit can be introduced before students have begun reading, after chapter 7 when Gatsby is revealed to be a bootlegger, or after students have completed *Gatsby*.

Consider the following guidelines regarding when to undertake the different activities:

Essential Question for Discussion and Writing	Objective	Suggested Timing	Suggested Rubric	Additional Research
A. What exactly did Prohibition mean? RI 1, 2, 3, 4, 5, 6, 8, 9, 10 W 1, 2, 4, 5, 9, 10 SL 1, 4 L 1, 2, 3, 5, 6	SW analyze the Eighteenth Amendment and the National Prohibition Act in order to understand exactly what was and was not illegal under Prohibition and then explore a newspaper article to understand how Prohibition affected New Yorkers' alcohol consumption.	Any time—this set of questions doesn't require any knowledge of *Gatsby*.	A	N
B. What's a bootlegger, and what does it mean if Gatsby is one? RL 1, 2, 3, 4, 5, 6, 10 RI 1, 2, 3, 4, 5, 6, 9, 10 W 1, 2, 4, 5, 9, 10 SL 1, 4 L 1, 2, 3, 5, 6	SW use their understanding of the National Prohibition Act and *Gatsby* to explore Gatsby's drugstore businesses and to analyze attitudes in the novel toward Gatsby and how he gets his money.	After the end of chapter 7 when Gatsby has been revealed as a bootlegger	A	N
C. Who is breaking rules and/or the law and getting away with it in *Gatsby*? RL 1, 2, 3, 4, 5, 6, 10 RI 1, 2, 3, 4, 5, 6, 9, 10 W 1, 2, 4, 5, 9, 10 SL 1, 4 L 1, 2, 3, 5, 6	SW analyze the characters' consumption of alcohol and adherence to Prohibition in order to reflect on the climate of privilege, corruption, and lawlessness in *Gatsby*.	After students have completed the novel	A	N

Essential Question for Discussion and Writing	Objective	Suggested Timing	Suggested Rubric	Additional Research
Class Activity				
Editorial/persuasive letter RL 1, 2, 3, 4, 5, 6, 10 RI 1, 2, 3, 4, 5, 6, 8, 9, 10 W 1, 2, 3, 4, 5, 9, 10 SL 1, 2, 3, 4, 6 L 1, 2, 3, 5, 6	SW individually compose editorials arguing for or against Prohibition based on President Harding's remarks about lawlessness in American society and consideration of the final events of the novel. SW then discuss and/or debate their arguments in small groups and as a class.	After students have completed the novel	Rubric included	N

NOTES ON THE READINGS

- Prohibition probably is most challenging because it is one of those historical events in American history that appears to be simpler than it is. Many students will have learned about the prohibition of alcohol, and they may be familiar with the association between Prohibition and the rise of organized crime. With *Gatsby*, it's probably more important that they understand the relationship between Prohibition and a general disregard for the law, although enforcement of Prohibition was meted out unevenly, with substantial penalties for violations for immigrants, the poor, and people of color living outside the privileged world of *Gatsby*.
- The first two excerpts are relatively straightforward, although the legal language of the National Prohibition Act is dense. The third excerpt is more challenging because of its ironic tone.

SUGGESTED MEDIA LINKS

- Ken Burns and Lynn Novick's PBS film *Prohibition* and the accompanying website offer a wealth of usable clips together with lesson plans and activities. "The Good Bootlegger," which is about six minutes, tells the story of one Oregon policeman turned bootlegger and offers an interesting counterpoint to Tom's revulsion toward bootleggers. "Satan's Seat" is a two-minute clip focused specifically on Prohibition in New York City. The website also has a photo gallery, and the Speakeasy Cocktail Price List is a useful visual to begin a discussion about the contrast between the law and reality under Prohibition.
- The first three minutes or so of *The Century, America's Time: Boom To Bust* (Part 1), produced by ABC News, also offer a lively general overview of Prohibition.
- A number of useful photographs and cartoon images about Prohibition and/or bootlegging, available through a Google image search, offer students an engaging entrance into the topic. For example, "Kosher Wine for Sacramental Purposes," "Bootlegger's Ball," "The Impact of Organized Crime on the City of Chicago," and "Throwback Thursday" all allow students an opportunity to begin to unpack the complicated attitudes toward and enforcement of Prohibition.

VOCABULARY WARM-UP

> **WORDS TO OWN:** ample, brisk, concurrent, construed, importation, intoxicating, jurisdiction, means, medicinal, observance, ratification, rites, saloon

Section A: Use context clues: Read the following sentences and use context clues to determine the meaning of the italicized words.

1. It is easy to get an alcoholic drink at the corner *saloon*, but far more difficult to get one at the library. Why do you think that is? What do you think is the business of a *saloon*?

2. *Medicinal* use of marijuana for easing symptoms of certain illnesses has gained broader acceptance, but recreational use of marijuana still is relatively controversial. What do you think is the reason for this difference? Do you support *medicinal* marijuana? Why or why not?

3. I find running to be *intoxicating*, and some research suggests that our brains produce dopamine during exercise, which creates a natural high. What activities do you find *intoxicating*?

Section B: More context clues: Here your task is to use context clues to understand the italicized word's meaning AND to practice your context clues skills.

1. The Eighteenth Amendment prohibited the manufacture and sale of alcohol as well as "the importation thereof into, or the exportation thereof from the United States and all territory subject to the jurisdiction thereof for beverage purposes." By *importation*, the amendment means

    a) sending out
    b) bringing in
    c) selling
    d) drinking

May be photocopied for classroom use. *Using Informational Text to Teach* The Great Gatsby by Audrey Fisch and Susan Chenelle © 2018 (Lanham, MD: Rowman & Littlefield).

2. Which word(s) from the sentence in Question 1 best help(s) the reader understand the meaning of *importation*?

   a) all territory
   b) subject
   c) beverage purposes
   d) into

3. The National Prohibition Act clarified the definition of "intoxicating liquors" by indicating that "The words 'beer, wine, or other intoxicating malt or vinous liquors' ... shall be hereafter *construed* to mean any such beverages which contain one-half of 1 per centum or more of alcohol by volume." The word *construed* is used here to mean

   a) dangerous
   b) constitutional
   c) guess
   d) understood

4. Which word(s) from the sentence in Question 3 best help(s) you understand the meaning of *construed*?

   a) clarified the definition
   b) by volume
   c) The words
   d) Alcohol

5. It is in the theme park's best interest to have an *ample* supply of bottled water for sale; on a hot day, it can sell a lot of water and make loads of money. The word *ample* here is used to mean

   a) small
   b) sample
   c) similar
   d) sufficient

6. Which word(s) from the sentence in Question 5 best help(s) you understand the meaning of *ample*?

   a) bottled water
   b) theme park
   c) a lot
   d) money

Section C: Sometimes common words are used in uncommon ways. **Use the dictionary** in order to understand the uncommon meanings of the italicized common words.

1. We might take the dog for a *brisk* walk if we want to tire her out, but what does it mean for a store to do a *brisk* business? How are the two different meanings of the word *brisk* here similar or related?

2. Usually banks are closed in *observance* of certain national holidays such as Presidents' Day. If New York City exhibits a lack of *observance* of a law, what do you think that means?

3. The United States is a country in which the right to practice one's religion and to perform the *rites* of one's religion are celebrated as fundamental to our national identity. How is the right to practice one's religion different from a religious *rite*?

4. Machiavelli is famous for saying the ends sometimes justify the *means*, although he didn't say exactly that. Some use his idea to justify questionable methods or unethical approaches to certain problems. For example, some thinkers have argued that international terrorism is such a serious problem that the United States is justified in using torture to try to address and prevent terrorism. These thinkers argue that torture is an acceptable *means* by which to achieve the result, or the ends, of identifying threats to the United States and protecting Americans. What do you think? Is torture ever justified as the *means* to an end?

May be photocopied for classroom use. *Using Informational Text to Teach* The Great Gatsby by Audrey Fisch and Susan Chenelle © 2018 (Lanham, MD: Rowman & Littlefield).

Section D: Use the dictionary to look up the italicized words and answer the following questions based on their definitions.

1. The Eighteenth Amendment applied to all territories subject to the *jurisdiction* of the United States. Which territories are subject to U.S. *jurisdiction* today? What is the consequence for these territories of being subject to U.S. *jurisdiction*?

2. In my family, my father and my grandmother have and exert *concurrent* power over me. This means I have to satisfy two sets of needs and demands. How do you think I can best cope with their *concurrent* demands?

3. Some people view a college acceptance letter as a kind of *ratification* of academic achievement and success. What do you think? Are you skeptical about the idea that college acceptance *ratifies* one's accomplishments?

4. Do you like a pair of jeans with an *ample* waistline so that you can eat a big lunch and feel comfortable, or do you prefer a snug pair? Why?

5. I try to speak carefully and cautiously so that my meaning can be *construed* easily by my words. Do you worry about the idea that others might *construe* or *misconstrue* your meaning? Why or why not?

6. In the beginning of the twentieth century, *intoxicating* beverages were consumed widely and regularly, often because they were safer to drink than water. Why do you think this practice changed?

7. The expression "there's no such thing as a free lunch" stems from the pre-Prohibition practice of serving free food (lunch) in *saloons*. These establishments were able to offer free, often very salty, food; can you guess how they made money? Given this history, what do you think about the expression? Was the lunch free?

May be photocopied for classroom use. *Using Informational Text to Teach* The Great Gatsby by Audrey Fisch and Susan Chenelle © 2018 (Lanham, MD: Rowman & Littlefield).

Section E: Practice using the word correctly by choosing the correct form of the word that best fits in the blank within the following sentences.

1. In 1972, both houses of the U.S. Congress passed the Equal Rights Amendment, but not enough states passed the amendment before the _____ deadline of 1979.

    a) ratify
    b) ratification
    c) ratified
    d) ratifies

2. If you deliberately ____ my directions, you have no one but yourself to blame for the fact that you completed the project incorrectly.

    a) misconstrue
    b) misconstruing
    c) construing
    d) unconstrued

3. Prohibition made the ____ of alcohol into the United States a crime; still, Canada became a regular supplier of liquor into the United States.

    a) importer
    b) importation
    c) importations
    d) export

4. Uneven enforcement of Prohibition in the Roaring Twenties meant that the rich could enjoy their ____ beverages at fancy clubs while poor people manufactured and consumed poor-quality alcohol in ways that put their health and even their lives at risk.

    a) intoxicate
    b) intoxicated
    c) intoxicating
    d) intoxicatingly

May be photocopied for classroom use. *Using Informational Text to Teach* The Great Gatsby by Audrey Fisch and Susan Chenelle © 2018 (Lanham, MD: Rowman & Littlefield).

5. ___ were not just bars; for many ethnic and immigrant groups, the neighborhood ___ offered alcohol but also functioned as a community center, a safety net, and a gathering place for social, economic, and political support.

   a) Saloon . . . saloons
   b) Saloon . . . saloon
   c) Saloons . . . saloons
   d) Saloons . . . saloon

6. Politicians can be determined to win elections by any ___ necessary; this doesn't seem a healthy aspect of our political climate.

   a) mean
   b) means
   c) meaning
   d) meanings

Section F: Vocabulary skits
Use the model sentences and definitions to understand the words in question. Create a skit in which you address the given topic. Every member of the group must use the vocabulary word at least once during your performance of the skit.

1. *means*—resources, agency, or method to achieve an outcome
   - Do you think the ends always justify the *means*, no matter what?
   - I don't think I have the *means* to endure another miserable year of bullying.
   - Negative advertising is the regular *means* by which political campaigns are conducted today.

Scenario: Create a skit in which a community gathers together to discuss the problem of drug use. Do they have the *means* to address the problem? How, according to police, teachers, clergy, parents, and students, should the community try to tackle the problem? What are the most powerful *means* at their disposal?

2. *concurrent*—cooperating, having equal authority, in agreement, happening at the same time

- If the school runs the sections of Spanish and Latin *concurrently*, then students won't be able to take both languages.
- Do you think a student-run dispute resolution group should have *concurrent* authority with the school administration in determining outcomes for student violations?
- If students run the student council meetings *concurrently* with the yearbook meetings, will they be forced to choose between activities?

Scenario: Create a skit in which two friends who have their birthdays on the same day plan their birthday celebrations. What will happen if they have their parties *concurrently*? How will their friends decide which party to attend if both are held *concurrently*? What other options aside from *concurrent* parties could they explore?

3. *construed*—interpreted, understood, took to mean

- Am I correct in *construing* your rejection of my invitation to the movies to mean that you are not interested in dating me?
- You can try to *construe* his intentions by reading his gestures and his facial expression, but you could also just ask him what he means to do.
- Because text messages and email communications make reading tone difficult, they often result in misunderstanding because someone *misconstrues* the message.

Scenario: Create a skit in which a group of students tries to *construe* the meaning of a vague text message from one student to another. First, create the vague text message (e.g., meet me later, I can't believe you did that, What?). What exactly is the writer of the text saying or asking? How, according to the group, should the meaning of the text be *construed*? Are there other details in the text that can help them *construe* the intent or meaning behind the message? How should the recipient of the message respond?

ESSENTIAL QUESTION: EVERYONE IS DRINKING, SO WHY DOES IT MATTER IN *GATSBY*?

Introduction to the Unit

The prohibition of alcohol was central to the United States of the 1920s. The three readings below flesh out some of the specifics of Prohibition. In the first, the Eighteenth Amendment, we see the broad and vague ways in which Congress defined and attempted to limit alcohol consumption. In the second, a selection from the National Prohibition Act, we see how Congress tried to create a system for the practical enforcement of Prohibition.

Finally, in an excerpt from a humorous article in the *New York Times*, we see the difficulty of that enforcement and the ways in which Prohibition instead contributed to general lawlessness and to the creation of a variety of illegal businesses, such as drugstores that produced and distributed alcohol.

READING #1: EIGHTEENTH AMENDMENT

Introduction

> **Reflect on the essential question:** What do you know already about Prohibition? Conjecture about how Prohibition could matter to the characters in *Gatsby*.
>
> **Reflect on the introduction:** Why do you think the nation decided to outlaw alcohol? What problems do you think Prohibition created? Why do you think the enforcement of Prohibition would have been difficult?
>
> **Reflect and research:** How do we go about amending our Constitution? Given what a lengthy, politically involved, and difficult process it is, what do you think about the fact that Congress tried and was able to pass Prohibition as a constitutional amendment? What does this tell you about how serious a problem alcohol was perceived in our nation to be at this time?

On December 18, 1917, Congress passed the Eighteenth Amendment to the U.S. Constitution. On January 16, 1919, after the amendment was ratified by thirty-six states, it took effect.

May be photocopied for classroom use. *Using Informational Text to Teach* The Great Gatsby by Audrey Fisch and Susan Chenelle © 2018 (Lanham, MD: Rowman & Littlefield).

The United States Constitution: Amendment XVIII: Prohibition of Liquor

SECTION 1
After one year from the *ratification* of this article the manufacture, sale, or transportation of *intoxicating* liquors within, the *importation* thereof into, or the exportation thereof from the United States and all territory subject to the jurisdiction thereof for beverage purposes is hereby prohibited.

SECTION 2
The Congress and the several States shall have *concurrent* power to enforce this article by appropriate legislation.

SECTION 3
This article shall be inoperative unless it shall have been ratified as an amendment to the Constitution by the legislatures of the several States, as provided in the Constitution, within seven years from the date of the submission hereof to the States by the Congress.

U.S. Constitution. Amend. XVIII.

Key idea: Look carefully at the language of Section 1. What exactly is prohibited? What is not prohibited? Can you see any issues with the language of the amendment?

Reflect: How long did it take to ratify the Eighteenth Amendment? How much time was allotted for ratification of the amendment? Why do you think Congress allotted this amount of time? How does it compare to the amount of time ratification actually took? Based on this, how politically popular do you think the Prohibition of alcohol was across the country?

Vocabulary: What does it mean for the article to be "inoperative" unless ratified by the state legislatures? If the state legislatures had not ratified the amendment, what would have happened to Prohibition?

May be photocopied for classroom use. *Using Informational Text to Teach* The Great Gatsby by Audrey Fisch and Susan Chenelle © 2018 (Lanham, MD: Rowman & Littlefield).

READING #2: EXCERPT FROM THE NATIONAL PROHIBITION ACT (THE VOLSTEAD ACT)

Introduction

After the states ratified the Eighteenth Amendment, Congress wrote and on October 18, 1919, passed the National Prohibition Act, also known as the Volstead Act. This law moved beyond a general prohibition of alcohol, called "intoxicating liquors," as enacted by the Eighteenth Amendment in order to create a complex system for enforcing the prohibition of alcohol, including defining what exactly constituted alcohol, "one-half of 1 per centum or more of alcohol by volume," and exemptions for certain uses of alcohol.

Reflect on the title and introduction: According to the introduction, how were the Eighteenth Amendment and the National Prohibition Act different?

From The National Prohibition Act (The Volstead Act)

An Act to prohibit *intoxicating* beverages, and to regulate the manufacture, production, use, and sale of high-proof spirits for other than beverage purposes, and to insure an *ample* supply of alcohol and promote its use in scientific research and in the development of fuel, dye, and other lawful industries.

Be it enacted by the Senate and House of Representatives of the United States of America in Congress assembled, that the short title of this Act shall be the "National Prohibition Act."

[From Title I: the section below clarifies the definition of "intoxicating liquors."]

The words "beer, wine, or other intoxicating malt or vinous liquors" . . . shall be hereafter *construed* to mean any such beverages which contain one-half of 1 per centum or more of alcohol by volume.

Notice that the National Prohibition Act immediately takes as its purpose both to "prohibit" and "promote" alcohol. What is prohibiting? What is promoting? Why do you think the Act focuses on these two seemingly contradictory purposes? What do these dual purposes of the Act tell you about the nature of Prohibition?

Key idea: The Act sets out to define intoxicating liquors. What element is central to the definition of such liquors? Use a dictionary to look up "malt" and "vinous." What is a malt liquor? What is an everyday example of a malt beverage? How is a malt liquor different from a vinous liquor?

May be photocopied for classroom use. *Using Informational Text to Teach* The Great Gatsby by Audrey Fisch and Susan Chenelle © 2018 (Lanham, MD: Rowman & Littlefield).

[From Title II: the section below provides for a variety of exemptions to the overall prohibition of alcohol.]

SEC. 3.

No person shall on or after the date when the eighteenth amendment to the Constitution of the United States goes into effect, manufacture, sell, barter, transport, *import*, export, deliver, furnish or possess any intoxicating liquor except as authorized in this Act, and all the provisions of this Act shall be liberally *construed* to the end that—the use of intoxicating liquor as a beverage may be prevented. . . .

SEC. 6.

No one shall manufacture, sell, purchase, transport, or prescribe any liquor without first obtaining a permit from the commissioner so to do, except that a person may, without a permit, purchase and use liquor for *medicinal* purposes when prescribed by a physician. . . .

> **Key idea:** What exemptions does the Volstead Act define in Section 6 for the use of alcohol? Why do you think Prohibition permitted these exemptions?

Nothing in this title shall be held to apply to the manufacture, sale, transportation, *importation*, possession, or distribution of wine for sacramental purposes, or like religious *rites*. . . . No person to whom a permit may be issued to manufacture, transport, import, or sell wines for sacramental purposes or like religious rites shall sell, barter, exchange, or furnish any such to any person not a rabbi, minister of the gospel, priest, or an officer duly authorized for the purpose by any church or congregation, nor to any such except upon an application duly subscribed by him, which application, authenticated as regulations may prescribe, shall be filed and preserved by the seller. The head of any conference or diocese or other ecclesiastical *jurisdiction* may designate any rabbi, minister, or priest to supervise the manufacture of wine to be used for the purposes and rites in this section mentioned,

> **Vocabulary:** The Act describes the use of wine for "sacramental purposes" or "religious rites." How do some religious traditions make use of wine? Can you give an example of the use of wine in a religious rite?
>
> **Key idea:** Given that the Act provides an exemption for the use of alcohol for religious rituals, what provisions does the Act make to ensure an adequate supply of wine for these events? What do you think of the way the Act connects religious leaders with the alcohol industry? Can you imagine any problems this connection might have caused?

May be photocopied for classroom use. *Using Informational Text to Teach* The Great Gatsby by Audrey Fisch and Susan Chenelle © 2018 (Lanham, MD: Rowman & Littlefield).

and the person so designated may, in the discretion of the commissioner, be granted a permit to supervise such manufacture.

SEC. 33.
After February 1, 1920, the possession of liquors by any person not legally permitted under this title to possess liquor shall be prima facie evidence that such liquor is kept for the purpose of being sold, bartered, exchanged, given away, furnished, or otherwise disposed of in violation of the provisions of this title. . . . But it shall not be unlawful to possess liquors in one's private dwelling while the same is occupied and used by him as his dwelling only and such liquor need not be reported, provided such liquors are for use only for the personal consumption of the owner thereof and his family residing in such dwelling and of his bona fide guests when entertained by him therein; and the burden of proof shall be upon the possessor in any action concerning the same to prove that such liquor was lawfully acquired, possessed, and used.

United States, Congress, House, National Prohibition Act. 1919.

Key idea: Section 33 discusses the possession and use of alcohol in "one's private dwelling." What does the Act say about such possession and use? The Act describes the possession of alcohol as "prima facie" or clear and plain evidence (evidence on the face) of a violation of the Act. But it also suggests that the use of alcohol to entertain "bona fide" or genuine, authentic guests is not unlawful. Does it make sense that the possession of alcohol in one's home can be both assumed to be a violation of the Act and not unlawful?

Key idea: The Act indicates that the "burden of proof" is on the "possessor" in a case of possession of alcohol in one's home. What does this mean? How is this different from our standard of proof in criminal cases: innocent until proven guilty? What sorts of people do you think would be advantaged and disadvantaged by this burden of proof?

READING #3: "MAKING A JOKE OF PROHIBITION IN NEW YORK CITY"

Introduction

Shortly after Congress passed the National Prohibition Act, it became clear that enforcement of Prohibition was going to be problematic. Enforcement varied by region and had a disproportionately punitive effect on people of color and the ethnic poor. The excerpt below from the *New York Times* article, however, published in May 1920, underscores how widely available alcohol was in New York City, despite Prohibition. The article also includes a specific discussion of the "drugstore" business, a particular form of the illegal production or distribution of alcohol, known as bootlegging, created by Prohibition.

Excerpt from "Making a Joke of Prohibition in New York City"

When is a law not a law? When it is a prohibition amendment—in the City of New York. Thus might be explained the lack of *observance* of the Eighteenth Amendment to the Constitution of the United States.

Be it known to the trusting and the unsuspecting, New York City is almost wide open today. For the knowing citizen it is about as easy to get a drink as it ever was in the days when the swinging doors of the corner *saloon* were the first sign of Spring. The point is that you must know the password, or know somebody who knows the password, or else take a chance on merely asking for what you want and getting it. In the last case you get it if the bartender thinks that you look as though you really want it, and need it, and can pay for it . . .

Otherwise law-abiding New Yorkers seem to be lacking in the proper respect for the dry laws.

Reflect on the title and introduction: What point of view does the title of this article suggest about Prohibition? What does the word "joke" in the title convey about the perspective and tone of the article?

Notice how the article begins with a question. Why would the author choose this approach? What do you think is the tone of the question here?

Key idea: Why does the article bring up the idea of knowing a password in order to get a drink? In the end, does the article suggest that it is necessary to know a password? What is important about this point?

Key idea: Why would Prohibition be referred to as "the dry laws"?

May be photocopied for classroom use. *Using Informational Text to Teach* The Great Gatsby by Audrey Fisch and Susan Chenelle © 2018 (Lanham, MD: Rowman & Littlefield).

It is no uncommon thing to hear that people are drinking more today than they ever have before . . . The question naturally arises, "Where do the restaurants get it?" The answer, "From all sorts of places."

BRISK DRUG STORE BUSINESS

Some of the doctors prescribe freely; others less so, others not at all. But most of them can prescribe. The druggists also have fallen in line to meet the popular demand for alcoholic drugs. They get their supplies from warehouses licensed to sell liquor for *medicinal* purposes. One warehouse in Brooklyn has changed its name so that the word "laboratories" appears on its letterhead. It recently sent out a circular to physicians in that borough telling them that it was in a position to fill prescriptions for any drinks appearing in their catalogue . . .

There are other shops of the same kind. Some sell their liquors for medicinal purposes, others for sacramental. The *means* may differ, but the end is the same. All are providing New York and its wife with spirits and drinks. And it is all done, apparently, in the face of popular approval, in spite of the fact that everybody knows and agrees that it is against the law.

"Making a Joke of Prohibition in New York City." *New York Times.* May 2, 1920.

Key idea: The final section of the article is subtitled: "Brisk Drug Store Business." What do you think is the relation between drug stores and Prohibition? If the drug store business is brisk, what does that suggest?

Key idea: What does the article suggest when it indicates that "druggists" have "fallen in line" to meet demand for alcoholic drugs? What is the relationship between this idea and the brisk business referenced in the subtitle?

Key idea: The article contains the line: "The means may differ, but the end is the same." Put this into your own words. Why are the means different?

Notice that the article refers to New York and "its wife." New York doesn't have a wife. What is the meaning of this expression? Do you think we would use this sort of language today? Why or why not?

Key idea: What, in the final sentence of the article, "is all done"? What does the writer mean that "it is all done" in the "face of popular approval"? Why does the writer emphasize that it is done "in spite of the fact that everybody knows and agrees that it is against the law"?

May be photocopied for classroom use. *Using Informational Text to Teach* The Great Gatsby by Audrey Fisch and Susan Chenelle © 2018 (Lanham, MD: Rowman & Littlefield).

CHECK FOR UNDERSTANDING

1. The National Prohibition Act indicates that no person shall "sell, barter, exchange, or *furnish* any such to any person not a rabbi, minister of the gospel, priest, or an officer duly authorized." The word *furnish* here means

    a) supply
    b) house
    c) decorate
    d) refinish

2. Which word(s) in the text best help you understand the meaning of *furnish* in the question above?

    a) duly authorized
    b) sell, barter, exchange
    c) rabbi, minister of the gospel, priest
    d) any person

3. Which of the following was NOT prohibited by the Eighteenth Amendment?

    a) the manufacture of intoxicating liquors
    b) the sale of intoxicating liquors
    c) the transportation of intoxicating liquors
    d) the consumption of intoxicating liquors

4. What is the purpose of the question "When is a law not a law?" in "Making a Joke of Prohibition in New York City"?

    a) To suggest that Prohibition was wrong.
    b) To suggest that Prohibition was not being enforced in New York City.
    c) To indicate that Prohibition was not the law in New York City.
    d) To ask whether Prohibition should have been the law in New York City.

5. Which question is unanswered by any of the readings?

    a) Why did Prohibition allow exemptions for medicinal and sacramental uses of alcohol?
    b) What constitutes an intoxicating liquor?
    c) How could people obtain alcohol during Prohibition?
    d) Did New Yorkers drink alcohol during Prohibition?

6. The main purpose of "Making a Joke of Prohibition in New York City" is

   a) to share tips for how New Yorkers could obtain alcohol.
   b) to debate the merits of Prohibition.
   c) to condemn drugstores for selling alcohol.
   d) to note with irony the lawlessness of New Yorkers in relation to Prohibition.

7. Which example from "Making a Joke of Prohibition in New York City" best illustrates the purpose?

   a) "And it is all done, apparently, in the face of popular approval, in spite of the fact that everybody knows and agrees that it is against the law."
   b) "Be it known to the trusting and the unsuspecting."
   c) "Where do the restaurants get it?"
   d) "The means may differ, but the end is the same."

8. In the *New York Times* article, the writer suggests the following about getting an alcoholic drink in New York City: "The point is that you must know the password, or know somebody who knows the password, or else take a chance on merely asking for what you want and getting it." The point of this sentence is to emphasize

   a) how hard it was to get an alcoholic drink in New York City.
   b) how easy it was to get an alcoholic drink in New York City.
   c) how you needed to know a password to get an alcoholic drink in New York City.
   d) the ways to get an alcoholic drink during Prohibition in New York City.

9. The National Prohibition Act indicates that "it shall not be unlawful to possess liquors in one's private dwelling while the same is occupied and used by him as his dwelling only and such liquor need not be reported, provided such liquors are for use only for the personal consumption of the owner thereof and his family residing in such dwelling and of his bona fide guests when entertained by him therein." Which of the following is the best paraphrase of the section above?

   a) It was illegal to possess liquor in one's home.
   b) It was legal to possess liquor in one's home.
   c) It was legal to possess liquor in one's home for the purpose of entertainment.
   d) It was legal to possess and consume alcohol at home, including with guests.

10. Which of the following was a potential consequence of the provision of the National Prohibition Act cited above?

   a) Wealthy people who had large homes in which they could store large quantities of alcohol could continue to drink during Prohibition.
   b) One could no longer entertain guests with alcohol in one's home.
   c) One could sell alcohol to one's guests.
   d) Churches could be used to manufacture sacramental wine.

WRITING AND DISCUSSION
A. What exactly did Prohibition mean?

1. **Discuss**: What exactly did the Eighteenth Amendment prohibit in relation to alcohol? What uses of alcohol were not prohibited? Why do you think the amendment was written this way? *Use Table 5.1 to record your analysis of the Eighteenth Amendment.*

2. **Discuss**: What exactly did the National Prohibition Act prohibit in relation to alcohol? What uses of alcohol are not prohibited? Why do you think the act was written this way? *Use Table 5.1 to record your analysis of the act.*

3. **Discuss**: "Making a Joke of Prohibition in New York City" indicates that "everybody knows and agrees that it is against the law" and yet "people are drinking more today than they ever have before." Discuss. Are you surprised that alcohol use, particularly among the wealthy in New York City, would have increased under Prohibition? *Use Table 5.2 to record the ways in which the article indicates people disobeyed Prohibition.*

4. **Write**: Using the three primary source documents, discuss what Prohibition meant in terms of the consumption of alcohol in New York City. Using the documents, discuss how and why alcohol use might have continued among the wealthy in New York City under Prohibition. What do you think about the fact that the legal underpinnings for Prohibition created so much ambiguity and leeway about alcohol consumption that noncompliance was virtually assured? *Use evidence from the Eighteenth Amendment, the National Prohibition Act, and the* New York Times *in your response.*

Tables are available for download at http://www.usinginformationaltext.com/student.

May be photocopied for classroom use. *Using Informational Text to Teach* The Great Gatsby by Audrey Fisch and Susan Chenelle © 2018 (Lanham, MD: Rowman & Littlefield).

B. What's a bootlegger, and what does it mean if Gatsby is one?

1. **Discuss**: "Making a Joke of Prohibition in New York City" focuses particular attention on the drugstore business in relation to Prohibition. How and why did drugstores do a "brisk" business during Prohibition? Which provisions of the National Prohibition Act promoted the success of drugstores?

2. **Discuss**: In *Last Call: The Rise and Fall of Prohibition* (2010), Daniel Okrent discusses the rise of Walgreens, one of the largest drugstore chains in the United States, which grew from nine locations in 1916 to 525 during the 1920s. Okrent writes that Walgreens introduced the milkshake in 1922, but he expresses doubt that the milkshake was responsible for the rapid growth and transformation of the company. Instead, Okrent cites a remark by Charles Walgreen Jr. about the danger that fires posed to the company. Okrent writes, "The elder Walgreen worried about fire breaking out in his stores, his son [Charles Walgreen Jr.] recalled, but this apprehension transcended concern for his employees: he 'wanted the fire department to get in as fast as possible and get out as fast as possible . . . because whenever they came in we'd always lose a case of liquor from the back'" (197). What is Okrent suggesting was responsible for the rapid growth of Walgreens in the 1920s? How does this story about the rise of Walgreens make sense in light of the comments about drugstores in "Making a Joke of Prohibition in New York City"?

3. **Discuss**: Early on in *Gatsby* and particularly in chapter 6, Nick, Daisy, Tom, Jordan, and other characters speculate about how Gatsby makes his money and what kind of background he comes from. In chapter 3, Jordan and Nick have a conversation in which Jordan doubts Gatsby's Oxford background, and Nick wonders how a man comes "out of nowhere and buy[s] a palace on Long Island Sound." Chapter 4 begins with the assertion by "young ladies" that Gatsby is a bootlegger who "killed a man." In chapter 6, Tom labels Gatsby a "bootlegger" and associates Gatsby with other "newly rich people." Nick refutes Tom, "Not Gatsby." Daisy then suggests that Gatsby made his fortune by building up a business in "drugstores." How do you think she understands Gatsby's work? What do all of these comments suggest about what it means that Gatsby is a bootlegger? How is that "profession" viewed by the characters in the novel? *Use Table 5.3 to collect and organize your responses.*

4. **Discuss**: In chapter 7, Tom confronts Gatsby with his history as a bootlegger selling "grain alcohol" in drugstores. In the ensuing conversation, Gatsby admits his involvement, and they discuss the imprisonment of Tom's friend, Walter Chase, as a result of his involvement in Gatsby's business. What is at stake in this conversation? Why would a friend of Tom's be involved in bootlegging? Why is this friend imprisoned but Gatsby is not? What do you think is implied by the reference to the bigger "something" that Gatsby is now involved with? Why do you think this conversation makes Daisy "terrified" and results in her "drawing further and further into herself"?

5. **Write**: How does Gatsby make his money, and why does it matter? What do the different characters in the novel think about where Gatsby's money comes from? How does Fitzgerald use the issue of Gatsby's "profession" to define Gatsby as a character whose wealth is fundamentally different from Tom's and comes from illegal activity? *Use evidence from the* New York Times, *the National Prohibition Act, and* Gatsby *in your response.*

Tables are available for download at http://www.usinginformationaltext.com/student.

C. Who is breaking rules and/or the law and getting away with it in *Gatsby*?

1. **Discuss**: Consider the various moments in *Gatsby* when alcohol is consumed. Who drinks? Who doesn't? *Use Table 5.4 to record your analysis of the consumption of alcohol in* Gatsby.

2. **Discuss**: Based on the provisions of the National Prohibition Act, which of the incidents you identified above represents a violation of the law? Why? *Use Table 5.4 to record your analysis.*

3. **Discuss**: Which characters in *Gatsby* engage in other kinds of lawbreaking activities, beyond the purchase or consumption of alcohol? What kinds of lawbreaking activities do people get away with in the novel? What kinds of lawbreaking are condemned within the novel? *Use Table 5.5 to record your analysis.*

4. **Write**: "Making a Joke of Prohibition in New York City" indicates that consumption of alcohol was widespread and made a mockery of the law. The broad disregard of Prohibition, however, reflects a larger pattern of lawlessness within the novel. Who in the novel gets to break the law without consequence and who does not? What kinds of lawbreaking are accepted and excused within the novel; what kinds of lawbreaking are condemned? What do you think is the broader message within *Gatsby* about the rule of law? What do you think Fitzgerald might be saying about the uneven enforcement of the law and the consequences to American society of an atmosphere of privilege and entitlement in which the law does not apply equally to everyone? *Use evidence from The National Prohibition Act, the* New York Times, *and* Gatsby *in your response.*

Tables are available for download at https://www.usinginformationaltext.com/student.

CLASS ACTIVITY

In President Warren G. Harding's 1922 Annual Address to Congress, he noted with dismay the general lack of observance of Prohibition and worried about the larger effects of a lack of respect for the law. Harding said:

> Let men who are rending the moral fiber of the Republic through easy contempt for the prohibition law, because they think it restricts their personal liberty, remember that they set the example and breed a contempt for law which will ultimately destroy the Republic.

Does *Gatsby* reflect President Harding's fears of a decline in the state of the nation? Are the events of the novel a reflection of the lack of moral fiber in and contempt of the law by the characters? Does the consumption of alcohol in the novel reflect a crisis in the United States and the moral failings of the characters?

Task: Write a newspaper editorial, along the lines of "Making a Joke of Prohibition in New York City," responding to both Harding's address and the deaths of Myrtle and Gatsby at the end of the novel. Use these texts and events to craft an argument for a) greater enforcement of Prohibition or b) the repeal of Prohibition. Stay away from general arguments about the dangers of alcohol. Focus on the issue of "contempt for law" and the issue of lawlessness in *Gatsby*.

1. **Discuss** in small groups. Share your editorials. Discuss. Which are most successful? Why?

2. **Debate** the issue as a class.

3. **Write** an individual reflection.
   a. Write a reflection in which you explain what you were trying to accomplish and the choices you made in composing your editorial. Explain how your editorial reflects your understanding of the conflict Prohibition posed for the rule of law in American society and the characters and events of the novel. Justify your reasoning with textual evidence.
   b. Reflect on the small-group and whole-class discussion. What have you learned? How have your views changed? How might you write your editorial differently? What might you change or add? Why?

May be photocopied for classroom use. *Using Informational Text to Teach* The Great Gatsby by Audrey Fisch and Susan Chenelle © 2018 (Lanham, MD: Rowman & Littlefield).

CLASS ACTIVITY RUBRIC

Category	4—Excellent	3—Good	2—Satisfactory	1—Unsatisfactory
Editorial (presentation of knowledge and ideas)	Editorial demonstrates strong and insightful comprehension of the issues at stake through ample, effective use of evidence from the novel and the informational texts	Editorial demonstrates solid comprehension of the issues at stake through frequent, effective use of evidence from the novel and the informational texts	Editorial demonstrates some comprehension of the issues at stake through occasional, though perhaps vague or ineffective, use of evidence from the novel and the informational texts	Editorial does not demonstrate comprehension of the issues at stake through use of evidence from the novel and/or the informational texts
Discussion and debate (participate in a range of conversations; present information, findings, and supporting evidence)	Outstanding participation in small-group and whole-class discussions, showing an outstanding ability to listen and contribute to collaborative discussions	Good participation in small-group and whole-class discussions, showing a good ability to listen and contribute to collaborative discussions	Limited or uneven participation in small-group and whole-class discussions, showing a limited or uneven ability to listen and contribute to collaborative discussions	Insufficient or unsuccessful participation in small-group and whole-class discussions, showing an insufficient ability to listen and contribute to collaborative discussions
Vocabulary (use domain-specific vocabulary)	Several "words to own" from the unit are used correctly in the editorial, reflection, and/or debate	Some "words to own" from the unit are used correctly in the editorial, reflection, and/or debate	One or more "words to own" from the unit are used in the editorial, reflection, and/or debate but perhaps not correctly or effectively	No "words to own" from the unit are used in the editorial, reflection, and/or debate

May be photocopied for classroom use. *Using Informational Text to Teach* The Great Gatsby by Audrey Fisch and Susan Chenelle © 2018 (Lanham, MD: Rowman & Littlefield).

Category	4—Excellent	3—Good	2—Satisfactory	1—Unsatisfactory
Individual reflection (cite relevant and sufficient textual evidence; improve writing and argumentation through reflection)	Reflection is clear, coherent, and shows excellent insight into all of the texts; reflection is outstanding and well informed by small-group and whole-class discussion	Reflection is solid and shows good insight into all of the texts; reflection is thoughtful and informed by small-group and whole-class discussion	Reflection is limited or uneven and shows limited insight into the texts; reflection is limited and unevenly informed by small-group and whole-class discussion	Reflection is unclear and/or incoherent and shows little insight into the texts; reflection is incoherent and not clearly informed by small-group and whole-class discussion
Documentation and style (in-text citation and works cited)	Reflection and editorial conform to the appropriate style guidelines (MLA) for in-text citation and works cited	Reflection and editorial conform with limited errors to the appropriate style guidelines (MLA) for in-text citation and works cited	Reflection and editorial attempt to conform to the appropriate style guidelines (MLA) for in-text citation and works cited but does so ineffectively or inaccurately	Reflection and editorial do not conform to the appropriate style guidelines (MLA) for in-text citation and works cited

May be photocopied for classroom use. *Using Informational Text to Teach* The Great Gatsby by Audrey Fisch and Susan Chenelle © 2018 (Lanham, MD: Rowman & Littlefield).

Writing and Discussion Rubrics

Rubric A

Category	4—Excellent	3—Good	2—Satisfactory	1—Unsatisfactory
Examples (cites relevant and sufficient textual evidence)	Essay uses and discusses thoroughly a wide range of examples	Essay uses and discusses a wide range of examples although the discussion of these examples may be incomplete or uneven	Essay uses and discusses some examples although the discussion of these examples may be incomplete or uneven	Essay uses and discusses a limited number of examples and discusses these minimally
Focused and cohesive argument (valid reasoning and organization)	Essay makes a focused and cohesive argument in response to prompt	Essay makes an argument in response to prompt, but the argument may not be fully cohesive or focused throughout	Essay makes an uneven and not particularly clear argument in response to prompt	Essay makes no real argument in response to prompt
Insight and understanding (determines the meaning of and analyzes text)	Essay shows insight into and understanding of the text	Essay shows some insight into and understanding of the text	Essay shows limited insight into and understanding of the text	Essay shows little insight into and understanding of the text
Grammar and mechanics (conventions of standard English)	Essay contains few errors in grammar and mechanics and they do not inhibit meaning; no patterns of error	Essay contains some errors in grammar and mechanics and they do not inhibit meaning; errors do not fall into patterns	Essay contains frequent errors in grammar and mechanics that may inhibit meaning; writing exhibits some patterns of error	Essay contains numerous errors in grammar and mechanics that inhibit meaning; writing exhibits several patterns of error

May be photocopied for classroom use. *Using Informational Text to Teach* The Great Gatsby by Audrey Fisch and Susan Chenelle © 2018 (Lanham, MD: Rowman & Littlefield).

Category	4—Excellent	3—Good	2—Satisfactory	1—Unsatisfactory
Vocabulary use (uses domain-specific vocabulary)	Essay uses precise, varied, and strong vocabulary; several "words to own" from the unit are used correctly	Essay uses some precise, varied, and strong vocabulary; essay attempts to use "words to own" from the unit, but these may be used infrequently or with limited accuracy	Vocabulary choices are sometimes imprecise, repetitive, and weak; essay does not attempt to use "words to own" from the unit or uses these ineffectively and inaccurately	Vocabulary choices are vague, repetitive, and weak; essay does not attempt to use "words to own" from the unit
Documentation (in-text citation and works cited)	Essay conforms to the appropriate style guidelines (MLA) for in-text citation and works cited	Essay conforms with limited errors to the appropriate style guidelines (MLA) for in-text citation and works cited	Essay attempts to conform to the appropriate style guidelines (MLA) for in-text citation and works cited but does so ineffectively or inaccurately	Essay does not conform to the appropriate style guidelines (MLA) for in-text citation and works cited

May be photocopied for classroom use. *Using Informational Text to Teach* The Great Gatsby by Audrey Fisch and Susan Chenelle © 2018 (Lanham, MD: Rowman & Littlefield).

Rubric B

Category	4—Excellent	3—Good	2—Satisfactory	1—Unsatisfactory
Examples (cites relevant and sufficient textual evidence)	Essay uses and discusses thoroughly a wide range of examples	Essay uses and discusses a wide range of examples although the discussion of these examples may be incomplete or uneven	Essay uses and discusses some examples although the discussion of these examples may be incomplete or uneven	Essay uses and discusses a limited number of examples and discusses these minimally
Focused and cohesive argument (valid reasoning and organization)	Essay makes a focused and cohesive argument in response to prompt	Essay makes an argument in response to prompt, but the argument may not be fully cohesive or focused throughout	Essay makes an uneven and not particularly clear argument in response to prompt	Essay makes no real argument in response to prompt
Insight and understanding (determines the meaning of and analyzes text)	Essay shows insight into and understanding of the text	Essay shows some insight into and understanding of the text	Essay shows limited insight into and understanding of the text	Essay shows little insight into and understanding of the text
Grammar and mechanics (conventions of standard English)	Essay contains few errors in grammar and mechanics and they do not inhibit meaning; no patterns of error	Essay contains some errors in grammar and mechanics and they do not inhibit meaning; errors do not fall into patterns	Essay contains frequent errors in grammar and mechanics that may inhibit meaning; writing exhibits some patterns of error	Essay contains numerous errors in grammar and mechanics that inhibit meaning; writing exhibits several patterns of error

May be photocopied for classroom use. *Using Informational Text to Teach* The Great Gatsby by Audrey Fisch and Susan Chenelle © 2018 (Lanham, MD: Rowman & Littlefield).

WRITING AND DISCUSSION RUBRICS

Category	4—Excellent	3—Good	2—Satisfactory	1—Unsatisfactory
Vocabulary use (uses domain-specific vocabulary)	Essay uses precise, varied, and strong vocabulary; several "words to own" from the unit are used correctly	Essay uses some precise, varied, and strong vocabulary; essay attempts to use "words to own" from the unit, but these may be used infrequently or with limited accuracy	Vocabulary choices are sometimes imprecise, repetitive, and weak; essay does not attempt to use "words to own" from the unit or uses these ineffectively and inaccurately	Vocabulary choices are vague, repetitive, and weak; essay does not attempt to use "words to own" from the unit
Documentation (in-text citation and works cited)	Essay conforms to the appropriate style guidelines (MLA) for in-text citation and works cited	Essay conforms with limited errors to the appropriate style guidelines (MLA) for in-text citation and works cited	Essay attempts to conform to the appropriate style guidelines (MLA) for in-text citation and works cited but does so ineffectively or inaccurately	Essay does not conform to the appropriate style guidelines (MLA) for in-text citation and works cited
Research (gathers and uses relevant research)	Essay incorporates relevant and appropriate research effectively	Essay displays appropriate research but does not incorporate research fully effectively	Essay displays limited research and incorporates it unevenly	Essays displays little research and incorporates it poorly

May be photocopied for classroom use. *Using Informational Text to Teach* The Great Gatsby by Audrey Fisch and Susan Chenelle © 2018 (Lanham, MD: Rowman & Littlefield).

About the Authors

Audrey Fisch is professor of English and former long-term coordinator of secondary English education at New Jersey City University, where she has taught for more than twenty years.

Susan Chenelle is supervisor of curriculum and instruction at University Academy Charter High School in Jersey City, New Jersey, where she taught English and journalism for eight years.

Together, Audrey and Susan also published *Using Informational Text to Teach* To Kill a Mockingbird (Rowman & Littlefield, 2014), *Using Informational Text to Teach* A Raisin in the Sun (Rowman & Littlefield, 2016), and *Connecting Across Disciplines: Collaborating with Informational Text* (Rowman & Littlefield 2016). They present their ideas about using informational text at conferences and in schools across the country.

www.ingramcontent.com/pod-product-compliance
Lightning Source LLC
Chambersburg PA
CBHW081817300426
44116CB00014B/2389